"Oh, Tilley," He Murmured, "It's Been Such a Long Time.

Can you ever forgive me?" But his lips wouldn't wait for an answer.

Tilley made no resistance but allowed herself to savor the kiss, to give in to the feelings of loneliness she had experienced ever since he'd left. This was the same David who held her in his arms, made love to her. This was the man she laughed with, danced with, worked with. This was the man she thought she'd lost.

"So what happened?" she asked when he finally released her.

"I don't know," he said, wearily, then with more conviction, he added, "No, that's not true. I do know what happened. I was absolutely terrified. I'm falling in love with you, Tilley, and it scares me to death."

SUZANNE MICHELLE

likes to think that she finds romance in her own backyard. Living in Houston with an extended family that includes four children, she loves to write and always uses a purple pen.

Dear Reader:

SILHOUETTE DESIRE is an exciting new line of contemporary romances from Silhouette Books. During the past year, many Silhouette readers have written in telling us what other types of stories they'd like to read from Silhouette, and we've kept these comments and suggestions in mind in developing SILHOUETTE DESIRE.

DESIREs feature all of the elements you like to see in a romance, plus a more sensual, provocative story. So if you want to experience all the excitement, passion and joy of falling in love, then SILHOUETTE DESIRE is for you.

Karen Solem
Editor-in-Chief
Silhouette Books

SUZANNE MICHELLE
Sweetheart Of A Deal

Silhouette Desire
Published by Silhouette Books New York
America's Publisher of Contemporary Romance

SILHOUETTE BOOKS, a Division of Simon & Schuster, Inc.
1230 Avenue of the Americas, New York, N.Y. 10020

Distributed by Pocket Books

ISBN: 0-671-49571-2

First Silhouette Books printing August, 1984

10 9 8 7 6 5 4 3 2 1

America's Publisher of Contemporary Romance

Printed in the U.S.A.

Books by Suzanne Michelle

Silhouette Desire

Enchanted Desert #29
Silver Promises #47
No Place for a Woman #57
Stormy Serenade #76
Recipe for Love #87
Fancy Free #106
Political Passions #128
Sweetheart of a Deal #152

Sweetheart Of A Deal

1

Thank goodness that's the last one!" Tilley Hart breathed a sigh of relief as she locked the door of the Chocolate Moose Candy Company behind a final departing customer. "What a madhouse! And it's only Monday. If business is going to be this good, I'm going to start needing longer weekends just to rest up." She ran her fingers through her frizzy red curls and smiled at the young woman who was taking the money out of the cash register on the counter. "You must be tired too, Amelia."

"I'm Rachel," the dark-haired girl replied, giving Tilley a quizzical look. The tall thin brunette wore her shiny black hair cut in a pageboy with bangs straight across her forehead. "Amelia left at two for her life drawing class. You must be tired. Usually you can tell us apart with no problem."

Tilley sighed. Sometimes she thought it had been a stroke of genius, hiring the Warren twins as comanagers of her store. But sometimes she thought it had been a mistake, especially when she got them mixed up herself. "Sorry, Rachel," Tilley replied, walking over and giving her employee an affectionate pat on the shoulder. "I know it's you. But it would be a lot easier to tell you apart if you'd dress differently."

Rachel looked up at Tilley with an expression of utter amazement. Her long bangs touched her eyebrows. "I can't help it if we like the same things! Looks and clothes are about all we've got in common, you know. Besides, Amelia can't talk for ten minutes without mentioning Billy Akers three times. Aside from the obvious, we're as different as night and day." She gestured toward her clothes—jeans, a pink cashmere sweater, and a string of pearls around her neck.

"I know you are," Tilley assured her. She tugged gently at the wide paisley cummerbund she wore as a belt with her yellow sweater and green corduroy skirt. "I'm just a little absent-minded today. I have a lot on my mind this week." She looked around the small candy store, her pride and joy. Half-empty glass cases held chocolate confections of every shape and size, including an entire showcase for the whimsical chocolate moose which was the store's namesake. In celebration of the coming Valentine holiday, there were lots of candy hearts decorated with brilliant colors and patterns of frosting, the store's best-selling item this time of year. Large old-fashioned glass jars lined counters and shelves, gleaming with hard rock candy in virtually every flavor and every color of the rainbow.

"I can't believe how much we sold today," she continued. "I'd better talk to Jacques about catching up tomorrow." She peeked through the large glass window that gave a view of the immaculate white kitchen, filled with copper pots, silvery candy molds of all different shapes, and a restaurant-size stove. In the middle of it all, a tall white-haired man was delicately licking a wooden spoon.

"You'd better be nice to him," Rachel said matter-of-factly. "It's Monday, remember. And he might be trying something new." Sometimes Tilley found it hard to believe that Rachel was the hard-nosed computer science major she made out to be. Underneath that veneer of economy and practicality there was a real heart of gold—and a lot of consideration for other people.

"I'll be careful," Tilley promised. "He won't get upset. Besides, it's about time for him to go home." She went through the swinging doors into the kitchen. "Hey, Jacques, won't Sybil be mad if you're late for dinner?" She looked over his shoulder to see what he was doing.

"Pooh!" Jacques snorted derisively. He was dressed as he always dressed for work—black pinstriped trousers and a white dress shirt with pearl cufflinks. Around his waist he wore a long white apron. "That same student is coming for a late lesson today. That boy has the worst tenor I've ever heard, and he thinks he's the next Caruso. Compared to my house, this place is peaceful."

"What are you making?" Tilley asked, reaching for the

spoon and taking a lick, her mischievous brown eyes on Jacques the entire time. She didn't really pay much attention to his complaint for it was a familiar one. Sybil taught voice and piano, and the Lebay household was filled with music all night and all day, some of it good, some of it not so good. In a way, Tilley had that to thank for having Jacques at all. After his retirement from work as a pastry chef at the Warwick Hotel, he couldn't stand the constant music. She hadn't been able to believe her luck when he'd asked for a job.

"Rachel said she thought you were trying something new." She quickly moved beyond range as Jacques shot out a hand in an attempt to reach the spoon.

"How do you expect me to finish this if you eat it all right out of the pan?" Jacques wasn't really grumbling, for he had long ago accepted the fact that Tilley's sweet tooth was virtually insatiable. "And it's nothing new. I just whipped up a batch of fudge for you. And some candy hearts. Don't you have a meeting here tonight? Those Green People?"

"Park People," Tilley corrected automatically, "as you well know. They've only been meeting here for the last six months, first Monday every month. And they're all gaining weight just because you like to work late on Mondays." She wasn't kidding. Several members of the group had suggested finding an alternate meeting place because of their low resistance to Jacques's tempting concoctions. But they kept coming back.

Jacques poured the candy into a shallow pan to cool and harden. "So all right, don't offer my fudge to those barbarians! Eating is one of life's greatest pleasures," he continued, patting his ample stomach. He paused, and Tilley waited for the inevitable question. "So what are those Green People up to now?"

"Park People," Rachel said matter-of-factly as she came into the kitchen on her way to the spacious adjoining studio, which was used as an office and work-shop. She sat down at the desk and started making some notes for her sister, who would be working the morning shift the next day.

Tilley laughed. They went through this same exchange every time the Park People met at the store. But this month she was really excited about the meeting, and for good reason. "We're trying to buy a piece of land in Montrose," she said proudly. "It's beautiful—about six acres and already wooded. There are incredible birds and trees there, too. It just needs to be cleared a bit and have a playground added, then it would be a perfect park. The land belongs to a family named Parker, so we're calling it Parker Park for the moment. There's just one problem, though." She frowned as she remembered.

"I bet it's money," Rachel called through the open doorway.

"Well, yes, but it's more than that," Tilley admitted, her brown eyes flashing. "It's David Danforth. He may have already bought the land. I've written him a letter asking him to reconsider." She didn't add that she had mailed the letter over two weeks ago, and only as a last resort after failing to reach the man on the phone.

"David Danforth? Danforth's Department Stores? Fat chance!" Rachel got up and came into the kitchen.

"Tilley, I think you've bitten off more than you can chew. When you're talking about David Danforth, you're talking about big money. Lots of it."

"So?" Jacques muttered loyally. "Tilley knows all about big money. Anyone who was a successful stockbroker—on Wall Street, no less," he pointed out, "has got to know about money."

"I'm talking old family fortune here," Rachel insisted, ignoring his comment. "I mean, I admire your civic involvement, Tilley, but I don't think you're going to get anywhere with that man."

"You never know until you try," Tilley announced, not giving an inch. "And I'm going to try. If he doesn't answer my letter soon, I'll call and try to set up a meeting." If he didn't answer his mail, she'd just keep calling until she got in touch with him. No businessman was out of his office all the time.

Rachel scoffed. "Good luck!" She went back into the studio and returned with a backpack over her shoulders and bicycle clamps on her straight-leg jeans. "I'm off to my computer terminal. Believe me, Tilley, when I make my fortune, I'm not going to open a candy company. Too many temptations." She grinned, grabbing a chocolate as she walked toward the back door.

"Stop, thief!" Jacques called after her, but she was already gone. He shrugged his shoulders in resignation and began to carry pans to the stainless steel sink. Tilley had long ago given up on persuading Jacques that he didn't have to wash dishes. When he worked late, he always left the kitchen neat as a pin, and he made sure that the two assistant cooks and the dishwasher who worked with him in the mornings did the same. She left him to it and went into the studio.

She crossed to her desk and saw a page of notes for Amelia in Rachel's precise handwriting and, next to it, a note addressed to her.

> Roses are red,
> Violets are blue,
> If we run out of catalogs
> I won't have any work to do.

She couldn't help laughing out loud. Pepper Malone came in each night after a shift as a bartender at the Plaza Hotel to take care of the mail order part of the Chocolate Moose business. He spent the rest of the time writing poetry, not that this was one of his best efforts. He'd had several of his literary poems accepted for publication, but he always wrote notes to Tilley in doggerel. She made a mental note to finish up the new catalog as soon as possible. The mail order part of her business was growing by leaps and bounds.

"Need any help setting up for your meeting?" Jacques stuck his head through the doorway. Tilley looked around, but everything seemed to be set. She had put out brightly colored metal folding chairs earlier that afternoon. All she had to do now was make the coffee.

"No thanks," she said, "but I appreciate the offer. Take a look at this." She handed him the poem.

Jacques read it and laughed, shaking his head. "That Pepper! What a kid!"

Tilley pretended to be offended. "Jacques, he's not a

kid. He's five years younger than I am, and I'm thirty."
She drew herself up with all the dignity her five-foot-six-inch frame would allow.

Jacques apparently decided to indulge her. "You're all kids to me, Tilley. And Pepper wears his hair in a long ponytail. That's hardly a sign of maturity, at least not in my book."

He had a point, she had to admit. "Well, thanks for the offer of help, but I think this kid can handle everything from here on out. Linda Baker will be over from Rice, and she and I can make the coffee. I'm just going to run upstairs and grab a sandwich and change. You go on home to Sybil. I hope her voice student's gone by now."

"If he hasn't, he'll be leaving shortly," Jacques threatened. "Enough is enough. Oh, speaking of enough, I'm coming in early tomorrow to get started on some of the things we're running out of. It looks like we're going to have a busy week." His blue eyes shone with the prospect of making more candy, for Jacques was a man who loved his work.

"It had better be," Tilley said. "We have two weeks before Valentine's Day. If last year was any indication, these will be two of the busiest weeks of the year. You keep those gorgeous candy hearts coming. We sold a lot of them today."

"You can count on it," Jacques promised. "Good night." He turned and went out the back door, locking it behind him.

Tilley looked at her watch and decided to take a break. Besides, she was hungry. She raced upstairs to her apartment above the shop and went straight to the refrigerator. After a few minutes' consideration, she cut herself a piece of cheese and grabbed an apple, taking them into the bedroom. She loved to eat, but there never seemed to be enough time for it. She went through her closet and pulled out a pair of dark green pleated corduroy pants and a rose sweater that brought out the red in her hair. The skirt and sweater she'd had on all day long bore the traces of too many taste tests. She looked at herself in the mirror, her brown eyes bright with contentment.

"It's really working," she said aloud. "I'm really here." Even though the Chocolate Moose had been open for two years and was already showing a profit, Tilley had to pinch herself occasionally to make sure it was all real. Who would have thought it would all work out so well? Certainly not her father! Harry Hart, a banker at the old and prestigious Texas Commerce Bank, had recoiled in horror when his daughter had told him her plans. "You want to what?" he'd said at first. "You want to throw away an M.B.A. from Harvard to start a candy store?" Her mother had only looked up from a law brief she was preparing and said, "Sounds fine to me, dear." Julie Hart had always done what she wanted to do, and she seemed to see no reason why everyone else shouldn't do the same. But as time passed and the business had proven itself a success, they'd come to regard it with pride.

Tilley was glad she'd stuck to her decision. The hassles of living in New York and the pressures of Wall Street just weren't what she wanted out of life. It all seemed so phony, so unreal. When she thought back to that part of her life, she felt that she'd spent all of her time talking on the telephone to people she very rarely saw face to face. Tilley wanted the real thing. She wanted to work with people, and she wanted to make things. She wanted a small business, and she wanted one in her home town. And she'd done it, she thought proudly, and without turning into a mogul like David Danforth who couldn't be bothered to answer letters or return phone calls.

Tilley had taken her hobby, making candy, and turned it into a profitable, attention-getting business. The small retail shop had been an immediate success, and she'd gone into mail order as a result of requests from out-of-town visitors. The month before she'd been written up in a gourmet magazine, and last week a New York publisher who'd seen the article called and said he'd like to talk to her about doing a cookbook. Her candy was special, the real thing in a world of cheap imitations, and people seemed to appreciate the extra effort that went into making it.

All in all, her life was going very well, though Tilley sometimes wondered how she found time for it all. "That's the problem," she said aloud as she walked through her living room. "There isn't time for everything. Sometimes there isn't even time to eat." She was heading for the refrigerator again when the doorbell rang, and reluctantly she hurried downstairs. Time to get back to work.

"Hi!" Linda gave her a broad smile from the other side

of the shop's beveled-glass front door. "I'm a little early." The older woman was wrapped in a cherry red cape against February's cold, and her silver hair was wind-blown. She stepped into the shop and immediately took off her glasses. "All steamed up," she explained as she polished them against her cape.

"Come in and get warm." Tilley ushered the sociology professor back to the kitchen. "You didn't ride your bike over here, did you?"

"You bet I did," Linda said proudly. "That's why I'm in such good shape for my age. Not like you young people who drive everywhere."

Tilley gave a rueful chuckle. "There may be a lot of truth in that, but I'll stick to my VW. It gets me where I want to go." The two women started making coffee for the meeting. "Who's coming tonight?"

"A good crowd, I think. People are really interested in Parker Park. I take it you haven't heard from David Danforth?" Tilley shook her head and Linda continued. "Well, we'll see. I'm pretty sure at least thirty people will be here, but with this weather, you never can tell. Not everyone's as loyal as you are, Tilley. And you *have* to come—we meet at your place!"

"Well, you said you needed a meeting place and I had one," Tilley pointed out. "But you're right. Having the meetings here does guarantee that I'll spend at least one night a week thinking of something besides candy. It's good for me. I want to make a difference with what I do. I want this business to make a difference in the communi-ty, and if it means being a meeting place, then that's fine with me!" She stopped, a little self-conscious at her own speechmaking.

Linda was quick to put her at ease. "Oh, your business has already made a difference in my community," she teased. "I'd say it's responsible for at least five new pounds on this very body!" Tilley gave her a smile as she heard the bell and went to unlock the door.

A group of people were huddled together for warmth against the cold, and Tilley greeted them individually as they came in. There were a few Rice students and professors, some parents from nearby West University, some people who worked at the zoo, other business-people from the Village—an assortment of concerned citizens. The meetings were always announced in the morning newspaper, so the organizers were never sure how large the crowd would be, but Tilley had gotten to know most of the regulars. She was proud of her involvement with the group, and everyone seemed to respect her; she was due to assume the presidency when Linda stepped down the next month.

Tilley was about to pull the door shut when a tall man put his hand on the doorknob, covering her hand with his large one. Startled, Tilley looked up into the most beautiful brown eyes she'd ever seen. For a moment, she forgot all about her other visitors. She hesitated a second, then pushed the door wide open, pulling her hand free.

"Come in," she said warmly, hoping her voice wouldn't betray her hesitation. "Glad you could make it. Have we met before? I'm Tilley Hart." She closed the door and locked it.

When she turned back to him, he was smiling at her, extending a leather-gloved hand. "Just the person I wanted to meet, Ms. Hart. I'm David Danforth."

Tilley froze, her hand clasped tightly in his. Now that he was inside the lighted store, she recognized him immediately from pictures in the newspapers. But no picture could have done this man justice. He was dressed in dark brown slacks and a herringbone tweed sports jacket. A white wool turtleneck sweater made his dark handsomeness all the more striking. Tilley guessed he was six feet tall, and for a moment she wished vainly for another six inches of her own—at least. But those eyes, those deep brown eyes, stopped her in her tracks as they moved from the tips of her fashionable leather boots to the top of her red hair.

Tilley flushed slightly under his scrutiny, feeling herself recoil from the boldness of his gaze as if he had touched her with more than his eyes. She tried to think of an appropriate response. "I'm *still* glad you could make it," she said in a slightly strained voice. "I take it you got my letter?" She remembered the angry tone of that letter all too well.

"It arrived while I was out of the country," he explained. Tilley thought he was being pretentious, but she was willing to give him the benefit of the doubt. It was a reasonable excuse for being behind with correspondence. "But I got back yesterday, and when I saw the notice of this meeting in the paper, I thought I'd better come defend myself. After all, it's not every day I'm accused of having no pride in my city and no sense of civic duty." He hesitated a moment, looking down at her. "I assume you'll correct me if I'm misquoting your letter, Ms. Hart."

By this time, Tilley had regained her poise and was not about to be bullied, not even by David Danforth.

"Oh, rest assured, Mr. Danforth," Tilley said icily. "It seems to me that you know it by heart—though I don't suppose that will make any difference in your thinking."

"I don't know about that," David Danforth said, an enigmatic smile on his face. "A beautiful woman can always change my thinking. Already I can see that I should have come to a meeting months ago."

Tilley was outraged at his presumptuous behavior. "If you don't mind, I'd rather not stray from the business at hand. And I think it's about time we joined the others." Who did he think he was anyway? "Now, if you intend to stay for this meeting, I'll introduce you."

She led the way through the store, determined not to lose her temper again. He was probably just trying to provoke her and then use that as an excuse not to cooperate with the Park People. "This way," she said from the kitchen doorway, noticing that he hung back a bit, obviously intrigued by all the equipment.

Tilley stood for a moment at the door of the studio, trying to catch Linda's eye, but it seemed hopeless. People were milling around, getting coffee and sampling candy, many of them looking at the designs for Tilley's new mail order catalog, which were tacked up on bulletin boards across the room. The Park People had become good customers for the Chocolate Moose, but for a moment Tilley wished they were paying more attention to the business at hand. She wondered what David Danforth thought. "Everyone," she called, "I have someone I'd like you to meet. This is David Danforth."

There was a sudden silence, and people stood there for a moment, conversations forgotten. Even Linda's eyes widened slightly as she walked over to Tilley's side and extended her hand. "Mr. Danforth," she said graciously, "how kind of you to come." The silence broke as everyone resumed what they were doing, a few of them seating themselves in the colorful folding chairs, others coming over to meet David Danforth.

"Let's get right to it, then," Linda said, and she marched to the front of the room to call the meeting to order. "Our first order of business tonight is to discuss Parker Park. Mr. Danforth, who has recently made an offer for the acreage, is here tonight, and we'd like to hear what he has to say."

David tossed his coat carelessly over the chair at Tilley's desk and stood there with his arms folded, surveying the scene. Tilley thought he looked like a study in amused arrogance. "I think I'd like to hear what you have to say first."

Tilley rose and stood beside Linda. It was time to bite the bullet. After all, she'd written that letter. "All right. If you don't know already, the Park People is an organization of citizens who are interested in acquiring lands for the creation of new parks in Houston, as well as working to preserve the parks we already have. It's shameful that a city of this size has so little public land, especially in the downtown area, where the last few available green spots are being bought up to be turned into parking lots, of all things." Her speech had been so impassioned that she had to pause for breath.

David's voice cracked across the room like a whip. "And what makes you think this particular piece of land is suitable for a park?" He made her feel as if she were on trial, but the expression in his eyes was not unfriendly, simply . . . interested. Or did she imagine that?

"This piece of land, which we're calling Parker Park, is perfect for a park," Tilley asserted calmly. "It's surrounded by an old residential area, and our demographic studies indicate that there are a number of children in the area, young children, in addition to the students at the elementary school four blocks away. There are already sixty-eight varieties of trees, many of them as old as this city, flourishing there. It wouldn't take much work to convert the land—only minimal landscaping and installation of playground and picnic areas. It also wouldn't take much money."

"Well, buying it will," David retorted quickly. "Land that close to downtown doesn't come cheap."

"I hope you realize that we know that already," she said defensively, her eyebrows arching. "And we're prepared to offer a fair market price, but we need time. What exactly did you have in mind for the land, Mr. Danforth?" Her words were a direct challenge, and she knew that the group was following the exchange with interest.

"Nothing at present," he admitted, much more openly than Tilley had expected. "I've been interested in that area for quite a while, and my lawyers had instructions to watch for parcels of land becoming available. I didn't even know there was an interest in making a park on this land until I received Ms. Hart's letter." He looked around the room at the sea of faces. "Quite frankly, that piece of land is not particularly important to me."

There was a rumble of whispers around the room. "Did you hear that?" "Do you suppose—"

Tilley took charge immediately, her clear voice bringing order to the room as she asked the question they were all asking. "Does that mean we can have it?"

David Danforth ran an impatient hand through his hair and looked directly at Tilley. "You can't have that land until you have the money to buy it. It's as simple as that."

"That's one of the reasons we're here," Linda interjected with feeling. "Part of the purpose of this meeting was to discuss ways to raise the money. We have the guarantee of matching federal funds, if we can just come up with half of the purchase price. But if you're going to buy it—"

David held up a hand in warning. "Now hold on there! I'm not sure I'm going to buy it. I just have the option, an option that I see no reason to give up at the moment. I'd be a fool to withdraw and then have someone else buy the land because you can't come up with the purchase price." He looked around the room. "Now, where are you going to get the money?"

The room was deathly quiet, and Tilley could feel David's eyes on her. She broke the silence, trying to sound more confident than she felt. "I'm sure we can raise it. We already have a good bit set aside for the purchase, but we need a lot more."

"Bake sales!" someone suggested.

"No, that would take forever," another disagreed.

"We could have a walkathon and—"

"No, everybody does that" was the disparaging reply.

The discussion raged on as first one, then another fund-raising idea was raised and rejected. Tilley thought of the long hours she'd spent writing letters to the City Council and researching various tracts of land, and she wished she'd been thinking harder about this. She looked toward the back of the studio. David Danforth had apparently gotten interested in spite of himself. He'd poured himself a cup of coffee and sat down, and was listening intently, helping himself to a candy heart. For a moment, he almost looked as if he were a member.

The talk about money went on for about twenty minutes before that deep voice made itself heard once again. "You people are rank amateurs!" he all but shouted as he rose to his feet again. "If you want to get anything done in this town, you have to do it with a splash. Get lots of attention, involve lots of people. At this rate, you'll be baking cakes for the next ten years and you still won't have another park to show for it!"

Tilley, as a fellow businessperson, knew that he was right. They needed to develop their plans further. She also knew that the moment was right. She had him in a corner, and she intended to exploit the momentary advantage. "And what would you suggest, Mr. Danforth?" she inquired in a deceptively sweet voice, hoping to draw him in.

He fell for it, not hesitating for a moment. "Do something big—something tied to a holiday—something that would bring out a lot of kids. People associate kids with parks. Something like, say . . ." He paused, as if considering the candy heart in his hand. He shook his head negatively. "No, not Valentine's." He looked up and around the room. "How about an Easter egg hunt? Easter's just around the corner."

One professor from the University of Houston looked genuinely befuddled. "How would an Easter egg hunt raise any money?" he asked.

That didn't stop David for a minute, Tilley noticed. If the man could do anything, he could think on his feet. "Charge admission!" he announced. "That means you'd have to have it in an enclosed space, though, so you could keep track of everything. A park won't do for this. Maybe someplace like Astroworld."

Linda spoke up in a practical voice. "But Astroworld's closed for the winter."

David brushed aside her objection as if she hadn't even made it. He seemed to be caught up in his own idea. "I could get them to open it for this. It would be good publicity for them. They could afford to run the amusement park for one day and donate the proceeds to this group. I have a few friends over there. I'm sure I could take care of it." He looked around the room, as if warming to the idea. "I'll get to work on it tomorrow and have my advertising and public relations people start working on a campaign." He seemed genuinely committed, but Tilley knew that it was easy to say you were going to do something. Doing it was something else again. Besides, there was still one unresolved issue.

David was about to speak when Tilley interrupted him. "Does that mean you'll reconsider your option on Parker Park, Mr. Danforth? Does that mean we can assume it if we raise the money?" She held her breath. Maybe she was pushing too hard.

He looked down at his coffee cup contemplatively before raising his eyes to hers with a sheepish grin. "Well, Ms. Hart, you have me there. I guess that's exactly what it does mean," he admitted. "If you can make this Easter egg hunt work, you can buy the land."

"It's not really very much time," Tilley pointed out. But she knew the condition was fair, and she was surprised he'd conceded this much.

"Look," David said brusquely, and Tilley was sure that he was talking directly to her. "You want to get something done? You do it in a big way. This time, it means you have to do it fast. I'm offering you an opportunity as well as"—he seemed to be considering it—"a lot of free advertising. I'll even donate the grand prize for the Easter egg hunt. You've still got to come up with enough Easter eggs to cover Astroworld."

She couldn't resist the challenge. "No problem there. You're sitting in a candy factory, Mr. Danforth. The Chocolate Moose can handle it." She thought ruefully of the busy weeks ahead, but she wasn't about to back down. She'd do it somehow. Even if it meant making all those damned Easter eggs herself.

"There you are!" David smiled. As if sensing the note of conclusion in his voice, the members began to break up into individual discussions, and finally people began to drift away after agreeing to meet the following week.

Soon only Linda, David, and Tilley were left standing in the storefront.

"I'll be in touch, Tilley," Linda said as she gave Tilley a hug before dashing out the door. "Thanks, David—for your openness and your willingness to help. You're a real shot in the arm for us."

Or a real pain in the neck for me, Tilley thought as she closed the door after her friend and turned to face him. "I never expected quite this response to my letter," she said lightly, wondering what he was thinking as he looked around the store again. He seemed to be taking in every detail.

"Neither did I," was his ironic answer. "In fact, I'm not quite sure how I got roped into all this. But it's a good idea and a worthy cause." He buttoned up his overcoat and drew what looked like a cashmere scarf around his neck. "But a deal's a deal, and I meant what I said about getting my ad people to work on this tomorrow. My schedule for Tuesday is pretty full. Do you want to get together after the store closes to work out the details? Say, eight thirty at my office in the Danforth's on Shepherd?"

Tilley felt as if she'd just received a royal summons, but she knew better than to turn it down. "Sounds fine. I know the store, of course. See you then." She moved back toward the door, but David made no move to follow suit.

He was still surveying the store with interest. To Tilley's amazement, he reached over and removed the lid of a glass jar containing more of Jacques's special candy hearts. Taking one, he popped it into his mouth, looking at her all the while. "You know," he said finally. "I think these are wonderful. I could sell a lot of these in my store."

She bit back her fury at his proprietary gesture.

"I'm sure you could," she said politely. "I sell quite a few of them myself. That one's on the house, Mr. Danforth. The next one isn't."

The point was well taken. David gently replaced the lid on the jar and took his time pulling on his gloves. "Ms. Hart," he said, equally politely, "you surprise me. I'll see you tomorrow." And he went past her, out the door, and into the night.

Tilley locked the door behind him and turned off the lights in the store, climbing the stairs to her apartment slowly, thinking over the evening. He wasn't the only one who was surprised, she reflected. She was surprised at herself. Maybe Rachel had been right. Maybe she'd taken on more than she could handle. She'd have to be careful with David Danforth, very careful indeed.

2

～○○○○○○○○○○～

Sure, Tilley," Amelia said softly, pushing a long strand of dark hair behind one ear. "I'll be glad to help. Just let me know in advance so I can get a little ahead with my classes." Like everyone else at the Chocolate Moose, Amelia had been delighted to hear that good things were afoot with the Park People, and she was repeating her offer of assistance with the Easter egg hunt before leaving for the day.

Rachel came into the room, heard her sister's remark, and let out a snort. "Sure, that'll be the day! You haven't been caught up with your studies in weeks. It's hard to imagine you being ahead in any of your classes." Rachel sounded genuinely peeved. Taking off her backpack and stowing it in a closet in the studio, she didn't so much as smile.

"What's this?" Tilley looked from one sister to the other with alarm. "Amelia, are you falling behind? I told you that working shouldn't interfere with your classes. If you need some time off, let me know." She regarded the young girl with a worried expression.

Amelia had gathered up her things and was ready to leave, but not before she gave her sister a look of utter disdain. "When I need your advice, Rachel, I'll ask for it," she said coldly. "And Tilley, I meant what I said about wanting to help. I think what the Park People are doing is simply wonderful. See you tomorrow morning." Without another word she left the room, and a second later they heard the back door of the store close.

Tilley looked at Rachel with complete astonishment. "What was that all about?" she demanded. "I've never heard Amelia say a cross word to anyone before."

Jacques stuck his head in the door and asked, "Is something wrong? Amelia doesn't seem like herself today."

Rachel sank down in the desk chair with a sigh. "Oh, I don't know," she said quietly, her face filled with concern. "I probably shouldn't have brought it up, but Amelia isn't putting a lot of effort into her studies right now." She absently thumbed through some papers on the desk. "Well, I'd better get out front. There might be a dozen people waiting to buy candy." It was obvious that she didn't want to talk about it.

Tilley would have none of that. "You sit right there," she insisted. "We'll hear the bell when someone opens the door. Now tell us. What's going on with Amelia?"

Rachel's big blue eyes filled with tears. "I don't know.

She's always made straight A's, but this semester she doesn't seem to care. She even skipped her sculpture class the other morning, and you know how much she loves that. It's Billy Akers. She hasn't been the same since football season ended."

Tilley bit her lip pensively and looked at Jacques, who shook his head and said, "The two of you must be the most beautiful girls at Rice. Neither of you should be having man trouble. Besides, you're too young for it to matter so much."

"I know that," Rachel agreed, standing up and pacing around the room. "I don't want to settle down, but Amelia seems to have her heart set on Billy Akers. He's all she cares about, and I'm afraid she's heading for a fall."

"Well, if she is, I'm afraid there's not much we can do to prevent it," Tilley said glumly. "But we can sure be here to catch her. Don't you worry about that." As concerned as she was, Tilley didn't quite know what to do. The problems of college students in love were far enough removed for her not to have a ready answer. "But if there's anything we can do, let us know," she told Rachel decisively. "And if Amelia needs some time off, let me know that, too." As valuable as Amelia was in the store, first things came first.

Rachel nodded doubtfully. "I don't think that would help, Tilley. At least being here takes her mind off her problems and keeps her from being too depressed. She'll pull out of it, whatever it is. I shouldn't have given her a hard time, that's all. It's just that—" The bells on the front door broke into her words.

Jacques looked through the kitchen window to the front. "It's just Pepper," he explained.

"Pepper?" Tilley asked. "What's he doing here? It's the middle of the afternoon."

"So what have we here?" Pepper asked, poking his head in the door. "Looks like a staff meeting. That's what happens when you work the night shift, I guess. You miss out on all the important decisions." He seemed to sense that he'd interrupted something.

Rachel excused herself, saying that she'd better get up front, and without looking at Pepper, she hurried out of the studio. Jacques and Tilley exchanged worried glances, but it didn't seem to be the time to talk about it.

"What was that all about?" Pepper asked, watching Rachel leave. She was clearly upset.

"It's nothing," Tilley said, hoping to change the subject. She was wondering what he was doing there. Usually she and Pepper only saw each other late at night, when he came in to work on the mail orders. It was unusual for him to come by on his way to the bar. "How'd you know I wanted to see you? I meant to leave you a note last night, but I was so busy—"

"I know," the tall young man said glibly as he took a seat. "Last night there was a Park People meeting and you forgot all of your concerns about business because David Danforth was here." He propped his feet up on one of the long wooden tables and gave her a superior smile.

"Must be true what they say about bartenders," Jacques muttered. "Who's been confiding in you now?"

Tilley too was curious. "Yes, who? I can't imagine that Linda dropped by last night. She was on her bike."

"No, not Linda," Pepper returned with a broad smile. "David Danforth himself! Sometimes he comes in for a drink after the store closes. Last night he was later than usual, and when I asked him why, he told me he'd been to a Park People meeting. Imagine his surprise when he told me he'd been here—and I told him I'd be here later."

Tilley returned to her chair and sank down in astonishment. "I can't imagine," she said drily. No matter what anyone told her about living in a big city like Houston, she knew at heart that it was really only a number of small towns all improbably connected. "I hate to ask anything more, but—"

"Don't." Pepper held up a hand in warning. "I take my bartending duties very seriously. In fact, I regard all confidences with the sanctity of the confessional. I will tell you that he was excited about the idea, and I think that the Park People have an influential new recruit, but that's all I'm at liberty to say."

Tilley knew better than to press her luck, but she did feel relieved. She'd spent more time than she liked to admit worrying about what had happened with David Danforth. The fact that Pepper knew and liked the man eased her mind a good bit.

"So how about the catalogs?" Pepper was saying, and Tilley snapped back to attention. "We really are getting low. If I run out before we get another printing, do you want me to send postcards, telling people we've put them on a waiting list?" He swung his long black ponytail back over one shoulder and tugged at his mustache thoughtfully. "Maybe I could think of some neat little poem or something."

"Please," Jacques groaned. "I don't think that would help business at all." He waved his hands hopelessly and went back to the kitchen.

"He might have a point there." Tilley laughed, and Pepper joined in.

"Seriously," Pepper began. "I'm not the best businessperson in the world, but it strikes me that the mail order stuff is getting out of hand. I have five full nights' worth every week, and I'm hard put to finish them all. That magazine article must have reached a lot of people."

"I know," Tilley agreed. "We've gotten an overwhelming response." Privately, she wondered why it was that everything seemed to start happening at once. "I'll get to work on the catalog this afternoon, I promise. Just as soon as I get through that stack of mail and pay the bills. I'll meet with you later this week to check on our progress."

"It's a deal," Pepper said, swinging his feet down off the table and standing up to go. "Oh, Tilley, about the Easter egg hunt—count me in. I'm not much at candy making, but I can sure pack and deliver. I'll even help you hide them. I think it's a good thing you're doing." He walked over to the door and turned around thoughtfully. "Hey, what were you all talking about when I came in? It looked awfully serious."

Tilley paused for a minute, debating whether or not to

tell him. Rachel and Amelia sometimes dropped by the Plaza to have a beer and talk to Pepper. Maybe he knew something. "It's about Amelia," she began, and she proceeded to fill him in.

"Hmmm," Pepper mused, one finger toying with his single gold earring. "I'll keep my eyes open. I'd noticed Amelia wasn't talking as much lately, but I thought it was a fit of artistic temperament," he concluded. "I'm prone to them myself," he added, giving Tilley a broad wink.

Jacques snorted from the kitchen, and Tilley realized that he was listening to every word. "The only fits you have, Pepper Malone, occur when you eat all the chocolate in sight," Jacques accused, only half in jest. "It's a miracle those orders ever make it to the post office."

Tilley laughed at the familiar complaint. She knew that Pepper was a chocoholic, but it was his only fault as far as she was concerned. Pepper lifted his arms as if to ward off angry blows. "I guess I'll have to be more discreet in the future," he laughed as he backed through the kitchen toward the door. Then, at the last minute, he reached for a candy heart and popped it in his mouth, making a hasty exit. "See you, Tilley!" he called over his shoulder.

"He's impossible!" Jacques furrowed his brow in a mock frown.

"Maybe so," Tilley admitted. "But he's all we've got. Now let me see those hearts you're working on. They smell out of this world."

The rest of the afternoon went by with lightning speed, and before she realized it, it was time to lock up for the day. Damn! she thought to herself as she totaled up the day's receipts. She had barely enough time to change before meeting David Danforth. The catalog would have to wait another day. She raced up the stairs and cast a longing look in the direction of her small kitchen. No time to eat—she'd have to grab an apple on the way.

She hurried to her bedroom and thumbed through her clothes rack impatiently, picking first one outfit, then discarding it for another. Nothing seemed right. She knew that it wasn't like her to be so concerned with how she looked. David Danforth was already making her uncomfortable and they weren't even in the same room yet. The night could only get worse.

She brushed her red curls and looked at herself. The teal blue v-necked sweater looked nice over the matching wool skirt, and she pulled on a pair of soft black suede boots. At the last minute, walking out the door, she impulsively grabbed a long black shawl and flung it around her shoulders. There! If she looked like a gypsy, so be it.

She munched on her apple on the short drive from the store to Danforth's. She had gone over the events of the previous evening in her spare moments during the day, and she had found that she was beset by questions about the mysterious Mr. Danforth. Why had he given in so easily? Why had he gotten so involved with the Park People's project so quickly? It didn't make sense.

Maybe it was an empty gesture on his part. Maybe he thought that no matter what the Park People tried to do, they wouldn't be able to raise the money to save Parker Park from development. Maybe it was a way of making them look foolish. Tilley knew that it was wrong to look a gift horse in the mouth, but she was curious about this particular horse's teeth. They might be sharp. And as much as she hated to admit it, even to herself, she knew there was something about the man that was different from anyone she had ever known, something that affected her immediately and intensely. She liked him, and though she'd be hard put to explain why, that frightened her.

She parked her orange VW in the store's nearly empty parking lot and entered the doors as a flock of employees were leaving for the day. Making her way to the store directory at the foot of the escalator, she saw that the offices were on the fourth floor.

Someone was turning off the lights as Tilley stepped on the escalator, but she still surveyed the scene with interest. It is truly a beautiful department store, she thought as she tried to remember when she'd last shopped there. Here and there, in the darkness, she could make out the forms of mannequins draped in the latest in high fashion. Then she remembered. She'd bought a pair of high-topped leather boots on sale. Last fall—that's when it was.

When she reached the fourth floor, she found virtually no one there. She looked into one office with the door ajar and thought she heard David's voice from another room. Following her instincts, she marched toward the sound. She stopped in the inner doorway, for there he was, talking on the phone. He smiled when he saw Tilley and waved her to a chair.

"I don't care what time it is in London," he said,

continuing his telephone conversation. "You let me know what happens with this first thing in the morning—my time."

He was completely involved, and Tilley took advantage of the moment to look around the office. It was both opulent and comfortable. Deep, soft leather sofas and oversized chairs formed a circle around a handsome mahogany desk. Paneled shelves lined the walls, and fresh flowers in glass vases stood on the desk and on the marble-topped table in front of the sofas.

David slammed down the phone, his thunderous expression changing to one of complete cordiality. "Ms. Hart," he said formally. "How nice to see you again." He leaned forward and folded his hands on top of the desk.

Tilley broke off her survey of the office and smiled politely. So, formality is to be the order of the evening, she mused. Very well. She could do it as well as he. "Mr. Danforth," she assured him graciously, "the pleasure is all mine."

"I take it you had no trouble finding me. You've been to Danforth's before, haven't you?" He gave her an engaging smile. "It would hurt my pride terribly if you hadn't."

"Of course, I have," she replied. "Is there anyone in Houston who hasn't?" There was something about his last remark that she found winning. She felt the same way about the Chocolate Moose.

"Well, I'd like to think that's true," he answered easily, then he fell silent, his eyes directly on Tilley. Now that the formalities were over, a sudden tension filled the air between them, and Tilley couldn't help but remember how they had parted the night before. "But if I had to choose one out of a crowd, I'm glad it's you."

Tilley wasn't at all sure how to answer that. For all she knew, he said that to everyone. Professional flattery. "Thank you, Mr. Danforth," she returned more casually than she felt. What was there about this man that made her heart race so frantically? "You're certainly a master at the personal touch Danforth's is so famous for." Almost immediately, she regretted her unaccountably flirtatious words.

He smiled, seeming to sense her discomfort. "In that case, why don't you call me David? The personal touch might make our work together more enjoyable, don't you think?"

Tilley measured her next words carefully. "All right, David," she said evenly, "and please, call me Tilley." Then, in her most professional voice, she said, "Shall we get down to business?"

"Something tells me that working with you is going to be a most enjoyable experience," he countered, watching her reaction. There was just a hint of a smile about his full sensuous lips. Then, suddenly, he was all business, as if he'd given fair warning and thought better of it. "Come here," he said almost brusquely, "let me show you something." He got up from his desk.

Tilley was almost relieved at his change of pace, though something told her she shouldn't let down her guard. She followed him into a pristine workroom with white walls, drafting tables, and long-necked lamps throughout. The tables were filled with an assortment of sketches, apparently the work of an artist in the

41

advertising department. The rest of the walls were covered with photographs, many of which Tilley recognized from Danforth's recent Christmas catalog.

"Oh, this is charming," she said as she picked up a sketch of a rabbit riding the ferris wheel at Astroworld. She was so immediately captivated that she forgot to distrust him. "And this is, too," she added, pointing to yet another drawing of a rabbit hiding eggs in a cable car. "But are you sure it's wise to start planning things around Astroworld?"

David gave her a self-satisfied smile. "I think they'd be disappointed if we didn't," he said calmly. "Especially since they've already agreed to let us have the park on Easter Sunday. They want to keep ten percent of the admission price for operating expenses, but the rest of the proceeds will go to the Park People."

Tilley was so astounded that she sank into one of the swivel chairs and spun around in it in celebration. Pausing self-consciously, she looked at David with a shy smile. "You really move fast, don't you?" she said admiringly.

"When I see something I want, yes," David answered in a voice that implied a good deal more. "Sometimes I succeed. Of course, that's not always the way it works. Sometimes it's clear that a more cautious approach is called for. Patience is sometimes a more difficult virtue," he said, smiling at her. "Don't you agree?"

Tilley had no intention of picking up on that provocative innuendo. "Oh, absolutely," she said innocently. He might be playing games, but she certainly wasn't.

David stared at her thoughtfully for a moment as if he were about to say something else. Then, apparently deciding against it, he started shuffling through the sketches on the desk. "Since patience seems to be the order of the day, why don't you see which of these you like the best? My staff artist didn't have much time, and he said if we came up with anything of our own, he'd try to get it sketched tomorrow."

The next hour passed pleasantly enough. Once he settled down to business, David Danforth didn't waste any time. Tilley was surprised by his eager interest in the project, and the longer they worked, the fewer doubts she had about his involvement. He asked her a few questions about the art work, and they went on to discuss the hunt in greater detail.

"It's got to be something more than an afternoon at Astroworld," Tilley mused much later. "That's not going to attract any special attention."

"That's why the treasure is so important. I've got something in mind, but it's just an idea right now. I think it'll be just the right thing to catch the public eye." He rolled his pencil back and forth on the desk top. "I know! We'll announce that there's a treasure and invite people to guess its location! We can publish a different clue in the paper every week and say that we'll announce the winner of the contest at the Easter egg hunt."

"The clues will be the most important thing in our favor. Whatever the treasure is, the clues will have to do the trick," Tilley remarked as she considered the idea, realizing how much work would be involved.

"Don't worry about that," he assured her, "if the treasure's grand enough, we'll have all the attention we need. We can tell by the number of guesses coming in the mail how people are responding to the ads. Then we can make some guesses about the turnout for the hunt. There'll be two things going for us—a treasure to find as well as the actual afternoon at Astroworld."

Tilley thought the plans were good, better than good, but something was nagging at her. She couldn't let it go. "It sounds wonderful, David, all of it." She hesitated for a moment.

"But what?" he prodded.

Tilley looked him directly in the eye. She had to get to the bottom of this, and it was now or never. "But why are you doing all this?"

David chuckled. "You just won't believe that I have any honest motives, will you?" He looked at her for a long, searching moment. "In a way, you're right, of course. No good deed is ever without selfish motives, I guess. I've got my reasons, personal reasons, and one of them is that I like children and wish I had some of my own. It's my way of getting attention, and it's almost as good as having a kid crawl up in my lap and call me Daddy." He smiled slightly, as much to himself as to Tilley.

Tilley didn't know what to say. She hadn't expected this. She had blundered in like a fool, finding fault and making accusations. "I'm sorry," she said, knowing how feeble it sounded, "I didn't—"

"Don't apologize," David said, shaking his head firmly. "I'd have wondered the same thing if I were you. It was a reasonable question. And I like the way you do business, Tilley. Straight and to the point."

Tilley flushed at the compliment and glanced down at her watch to avoid David's intense gaze. It was already after ten. As if in sympathy, her stomach began to rumble, and there was no way she could cover the sound.

"Oh, my gosh," David said, as if he'd just remembered his manners. "You haven't had dinner." It was a simple statement of fact. "We'll take care of that right now."

Tilley started to protest, but she sensed immediately that it wouldn't do any good. David was already through the door, back in his office, reaching into the paneled shelves for a few odds and ends—a checked red and white tablecloth of heavy cotton, a corkscrew, two crystal wineglasses, and a can opener. Tilley watched in complete amazement as he reached into a cleverly concealed refrigerator and pulled out a bottle of wine.

"What on earth are you doing?" Tilley asked, completely baffled.

"Dinner's coming right up," he promised as he gave her the wine to carry. He led her out the door and down the now still escalator to the third floor. "Here's the kitchen of the restaurant," he explained unnecessarily as he led her through a large room filled with stacked chairs and tables to some swinging doors at the back. He rummaged around until he found a loaf of French bread, a knife, and some napkins. "Mmmm, this looks good," he murmured as he gathered up some pears and two dishes of what looked like a delicate custard and balanced them on top of the plates he was carrying. "I think this has the makings of a memorable dinner," he commented wryly when Tilley reached over to help him carry some things.

"I should say so!" Tilley wanted to stop this, but she knew they had passed the point of no return. And as much as she hated seeing him go to all this trouble on her behalf, she had to admit that it was nice to be fussed over.

She followed him down the steps of the escalator to the second floor. "Wait here!" he commanded, and he plunged through the darkness. A few seconds later, an island of light appeared across the room, and Tilley walked toward it, knowing full well where she was.

"I must say," she teased lightly, as David spread the tablecloth on the carpet, "this certainly seems appropriate. Do you have dinner in the gourmet section of Danforth's every night?"

"No," he said a bit sheepishly, "but you're right—it is appropriate. I do like to try things out now and then. It just occurred to me when I heard your stomach growling."

Tilley bowed her head and began to arrange things on the cloth while trying to hide the flush of crimson rising to her cheeks. David went over to a display case and started pulling things off the shelves. "This pâté is supposed to be good," he said, reading the colorful label of a French import item. "Might as well try it out and see." He searched the shelves, pulling down tins of Greek olives, jars of green cornichons and yellow mustards, and boxes of English crackers. "Now, let's see what we've got here." He got busy with the opener and started passing things to Tilley.

"Mmmm, this is great," she murmured appreciatively, spreading pâté on the French bread and sampling a pickle. "Glad you decided to have a tasting session."

"Hey, make yourself useful," David said. "Are you any good with a corkscrew?"

Tilley rose to the challenge. "The best," she assured him, and she set about opening the bottle of wine. "I assume this is going to be a working picnic."

"Oh, I don't know." David gave her a sharp look as he accepted the glass of wine she'd poured him. "All work and no play . . . besides, I think we've done all we can about the Easter egg hunt for the moment. I'll have to come up with the treasure, but I think I can handle it. And you've got to come up with a lot of candy eggs. Of the two of us, I'd say you've gotten the worse end of the deal."

Tilley didn't like the implication. "I can handle it," she said a trifle defensively. "It's a lot of work, but my staff is behind the project all the way, and I don't foresee any problems." She wanted to show him that she could handle her business as well as he could handle his.

He didn't press the point. "How did someone with an M.B.A. from Harvard end up running such a classy candy store?" he asked conversationally, catching her off guard.

Tilley caught her breath. How did he know so much about her? Had Pepper—?

David seemed to read her thoughts. He shrugged. "I had to know the story behind such remarkable candy," he explained. "I asked around. You've made something of a name for yourself in this town. Not that I'm surprised," he said offhandedly. "Candy like that attracts attention."

"Oh?" Tilley asked, sensing that he had more to say.

"I sent my secretary to the Chocolate Moose this morning with instructions to bring back a little of everything." He sounded as if he were making a confession.

"You did what?" Tilley asked, laughingly surprised.

"Well, you told me I had to pay for it," he admitted a little sheepishly. "So I bought some."

"And?" Tilley found she was holding her breath.

"Oh, don't be so coy," David said, almost impatiently. "It's great—all of it. The chocolate moose are wonderful."

In spite of herself, Tilley was pleased. She sipped her wine slowly. "You've just made my whole day," she said softly. Suddenly, she was a little bashful.

David grinned. "In that case, satisfy my curiosity. I know some of the facts, but I want the inside story—what no one else knows." His boyish eagerness was irresistible.

Tilley found that she wanted to tell him why she'd left Wall Street, why she'd decided to start all over again. His earlier candor made it easy for her to confide in him, and before she knew it, she'd told him everything there was to tell. "I got tired of the rat race," she finally summed up, "and I wanted to be my own boss."

"That's quite a story," David said with real admiration. "I inherited all this," he explained with a wave of his hand, "and I do a good job of running it, if I do say so myself. But I didn't start it from scratch. You did, and I admire that." And it was clear that he meant what he said.

The tension that had plagued them earlier seemed to vanish, and Tilley found herself asking questions about Danforth's. "It can't be as easy as you make it look," she prompted with real interest.

David chuckled ruefully. "No, it's not easy. And I spent the early part of my life running away from this store. I told my father I would never work in Danforth's—I thought I'd like to be an English professor, a scholar. But I couldn't stay away from the place. When I got out of school, I went to Harrod's in London to apprentice, which is why I suppose I'm dying to open my store in London now. Once retail gets in your blood, it's like a fever, it's something you just can't get out. There's the wonderful aspect of risk and the excitement of never knowing who'll walk through the door of your store—or if anyone will at all. You know how that goes."

"Sure do," Tilley smiled, identifying with his words. "I remember the day the Chocolate Moose opened. I never panicked on Wall Street quite the way I did then. And to think I left New York to come home to Houston and have a quiet life as a shopkeeper. It doesn't quite work that way, does it?" Her brown eyes met his in a look of perfect understanding.

"No, it doesn't," David agreed. He reached for the bottle of wine and poured himself another glass, stretching his long legs out on the floor as if he were really at a picnic. "This sort of business changes you, though. It was certainly the end of my marriage."

Tilley was touched by this admission, though she covered her emotion by reaching for an olive. This was a delicate moment—she didn't want to press him, but she didn't want to seem indifferent. "Do you want to talk about it?"

"I'm surprised you don't know about it already. It seems like everyone else does," he replied with sudden vehemence. "Toni married me for my money, of course, never stopping to think that I liked working for it as much as she liked spending it. She couldn't stand it that I spent so much time at the store. She expected the business to run itself. As strange as it sounds, I think she was jealous of Danforth's." He shook his head. "Maybe I'm not being fair to her. I don't know. Anyway, we decided to go our separate ways. She's remarried now—an Italian count who doesn't work for a living—and seems to have found what she's always wanted. I visit them occasionally. It's very friendly—perfectly civilized—polo matches and all that."

"Do you still love her?" Tilley asked softly.

David laughed, and it was a real laugh, no sarcasm. "No, Tilley, I'm not sure I ever did. We got together because everyone expected it of us, I think. We're good friends now—and that's something we never were before. I guess what still bothers me is that I seem to be following in my mother's footsteps. She's been married three times already. I always thought I wouldn't get married until I'd found the real thing. Now that I've failed once, I don't think I'm likely to try again."

Tilley was comfortably silent. There didn't seem to be

anything to say, or the need to say anything for that matter.

David twirled his wineglass between his fingers. "But what about you? I should think you'd have broken a few hearts in your time."

Tilley blushed furiously. "Oh, I wouldn't say that. Not that there hasn't been an occasional chance. I just never seem to find the time. I was pretty caught up in work the whole time I was in New York, and since I've been here, I've spent all my time working on the Chocolate Moose. I'll get around to it when I'm ready. Right now I have more important things to do."

David took that as his cue. "Right! Like making the best candy in the world and saving parks." He stood up and began gathering up the picnic things. "I'm sorry I've taken so much of your time."

Tilley sensed that he was regretting his openness. She began stacking their plates and packing up the food. "I'm the one who should be saying that, not you," she pointed out. "The Park People really appreciate what you're doing—and so do I," she added. "And thanks for dinner, too. It was delightful." She glanced at her watch. "Now, if I don't get going, I'm going to turn into a pumpkin any minute. And so are you."

"I suppose you're right," David said, glancing at his own watch. "It really is late. I'll just call someone from maintenance to come and clean up this picnic. Can't have the customers coming in and finding leftovers all over the place in the morning, can we?"

Tilley was horror-stricken. "No, no, don't do that. I'll

help you," she said, suiting action to the word. "We can have this cleaned up in no time." David tried to rebuff her offer, but Tilley was adamant, and for the next few minutes they worked together silently and rapidly.

"The kitchen staff will know what I was up to," David told her as he washed the last plate in the kitchen.

"I thought this was your first picnic in the gourmet section," Tilley reminded him archly.

"Oh, it was," David said, "but sometimes I come down and raid the refrigerator when I'm working late. The chef even leaves me little notes taped to dishes, like 'Try this' or 'Don't touch that.' Keeps him on his toes, I think."

"I'm sure it does," Tilley agreed, thinking of Pepper's tendency to raid the kitchen when he was working late. "I may have to try that myself. Can't have everyone eating up all the Valentine candy."

David hung a dish towel over a rack and turned toward her, a light burning in his dark eyes. "Valentine's Day! I should have thought of this sooner!"

Tilley felt a sense of foreboding. It looked as though David was coming up with another one of his famous ideas. "Thought of what?" she asked warily.

"My Valentine's Day ball," he said with enthusiasm. "I always have a dance at the house on Valentine's Day. You'll have to come. I'll invite all the Park People! We'll announce the details of the Easter egg hunt there—it'll be great for publicity. Don't you think it's a good idea?"

Tilley groaned inwardly. A Valentine's Day ball was the last thing she needed. By the time the holiday was over, she was usually ready to collapse into a heap. "How do you think it'll be good publicity, David? Isn't it just a party?"

He pretended to look offended, though Tilley could see a smile lurking at the corners of his mouth. "I'd like to think it's not just a party," he said.

"I didn't mean it that way," she said apologetically.

"I know it." David leaned over and squeezed her hand. The slight pressure warmed her through and through, though Tilley was quick to withdraw. "But it's more of a business occasion. I get rid of all my social obligations in one fell swoop. Most of the Chamber of Commerce will be there—and a lot of politicians, to boot. It'll be a great opportunity for the Park People to make contact with future supporters. And announcing the Easter egg hunt will make it more serious. If we could do that, I'd almost look forward to having the damned thing."

"Well, since you put it that way—" Tilley began.

"Great! Then it's all settled." David wasn't going to give her a chance to say no. He smiled down at her, his dark brown eyes filled with affection.

Tilley was suddenly very aware of how alone they were in the empty store, and she lowered her lashes against the intimacy of his gaze. "I'll call the Park People tomorrow," she said, more stiffly than she had intended. "But right now, I've got to get home. It's really very late." Hoping her voice didn't betray her sense of vulnerability, she quickly headed in the direction of the escalator.

If David noticed her withdrawal, he made no comment as he walked her out into the chilly night and stood a moment by her orange VW. He looked around at the black sky. "I should have come to fetch you," he said. "I don't like the idea of your going back to an empty place this late."

"It's better this way," Tilley said absently, glad she had driven herself. She wrapped her shawl around her as protection from the cold. "And I won't be by myself. Pepper will be there."

"Pepper Malone?" David asked sharply. "He told me he worked there, but it's after midnight."

Tilley laughed. "Pepper comes in to work on the mail orders after the bar closes. He leaves sometime in the wee hours and goes home to sleep, though I don't think he gets much of that. Mornings he writes poetry."

David nodded, his eyes meeting hers, a challenge made. "Pepper's a lucky man, getting to see you every night. Though it's a strange way to run a business, I must say."

He moved closer, and for one frightening moment Tilley thought he was going to kiss her. Part of her wanted him to and part of her wanted to run, to get away from this man as fast as she could. The moonlight bathed them in silver for a single instant, and David was just leaning forward when Tilley reached for the door handle and got into the car.

She smiled at him sweetly as she rolled down the window to say goodbye. "It may be a strange way to do business," she admitted, "but it's my business and you seem pretty interested in it."

"Oh, I'm interested all right," David assured her. "I'm interested in everything about you, Tilley Hart." He leaned down so that his face was close to hers. "And I meant what I said last night about selling your candy. I could make you an international sensation practically overnight. Don't forget—the London store will be opening next fall."

"Maybe some day," she mused, "but not now." She turned on the engine.

"We'll talk about it," David promised. "I'll make certain of it."

She was sure he would. And driving home that night, she knew that some part of her mind was already on full alert. She wasn't at all sure that she liked being the object of his close attention. Or maybe she liked it too much.

3

Tilley studied her reflection in the mirror, wondering how on earth she'd gotten herself tangled up with the likes of David Danforth. A Valentine's Day ball, indeed. A showcase for David Danforth was more like it! Oh, stop it, she told herself harshly, thinking of the unexpectedly gentle man she'd picnicked with in the middle of Danforth's. He's not like that at all, and you know it. You're just in a bad mood because you're nervous.

She put her hands on her hips and turned slightly. Her long black velvet skirt was certainly elegant enough, with its white silk blouse and red satin bow at the neck. She tugged at the bow, straightening it, yet pleased with the color. Her red hair was pulled back on either side with silver combs, and she had decided on just a smidgen of makeup—a touch of soft pink blush, some brown eye

shadow, and a new amber shade of lipstick that comple-
mented her red hair.

She picked up a hairbrush and gently worked with the
frizzy curls, giving her hair a soft but pert look. It really
was a business party, she reminded herself, and it would
do a lot of good for the Park People. Business was
business—especially with David. Danforth's is his life, she
told herself firmly, and don't you forget it. In spite of her
best efforts not to succumb to the tumultuous feelings he
aroused in her, she found herself drawn to him as if he
were a magnet, she a stray piece of metal. She had never
been so physically—and emotionally—attracted to anyone before, and she was determined not to let it disrupt
her life.

Just at that moment she heard the back door slam
downstairs, and a few seconds later, Pepper's familiar
"Hey, up there!" drifted up the stairs.

She hurried through the bedroom to the living room.
"Be right down, Pepper," she called. "I'm almost
ready." Quickly she looked around the small but tasteful-
ly decorated room. The walls were lined with bookcases
filled with books that reflected her yen for fine literature,
and a white dhurrie rug covered most of the highly
polished hardwood floor. A long low sofa covered in a
pale blue chintz had contemporary lines that matched the
glass and chrome coffee table. Large white pillows neatly
trimmed with navy blue piping were tucked under the
glass-topped table, ready for company. Two white over-
stuffed chairs that matched the pillows flanked either side
of the sofa and completed the ensemble. Everything was
in impeccable order, and Tilley felt a momentary urge to

stay here—not to leave the one place where she felt comfortable and safe.

Trying to shake off the feeling, she walked through the room to the tiny but efficient kitchen. Satisfied that all was in order there, too, she hurried back to the bedroom to pick up her short black velvet jacket and a beaded evening bag. One last glance in the mirror and a dab of French perfume were all she needed before going down to talk to Pepper. She wanted to give herself plenty of time for that, and she knew that the ball started at eight thirty. She had a vague idea where David's house was, and she didn't want to get there too early.

"Hi," she said, finding Pepper in the studio already packing wrapped chocolate moose in the colorful boxes they used for shipping. His long, slender hands really did look like they belonged to a poet, not to someone who worked in a candy company. She smiled at the thought, and Pepper grinned back without knowing the joke, self-consciously flipping his long black ponytail over one shoulder before reaching for more packing tape.

When he'd finished the job, he looked her over and gave a long low whistle of admiration. "That is some outfit! You're going to knock 'em dead, Tilley."

She flushed slightly at his approval, though not without some pleasure. "That's not exactly the effect I had in mind," she said lightheartedly, hoping that Pepper couldn't see how nervous she was. "I'd settle for turning a few heads. And making some good contacts for the Park People. Maybe even enticing some new customers to the Chocolate Moose."

"Well, you don't have a thing to worry about," Pepper

assured her, moving the package aside and leaning against the table on his elbows.

Tilley put her jacket on the table and pulled up a chair, hooking her high-heeled black pumps over the bottom rung. "Thanks, Pepper," she said gratefully, though her mind was already off on another subject. "Remember our talk about the Easter egg hunt?"

Pepper shrugged casually. "Sure—and I said I'd do anything I could to help. But I don't think Jacques is going to let me near the kitchen," he added with a mischievous look.

"Not that I blame him," Tilley laughed, as Pepper reached into a pocket and pulled out a bag of chocolate drops. "But seriously, I do need your help. I've thought of the one thing you could do to really help out." She gave him all the details of the plans she and David had made. "The tricky part will be the clues that will go in the newspaper. They can't be too obvious or the hunt won't be a challenge. And the solution can't be too hard or we won't have a winner. So"—she held up her hands—"you can see the problems."

"Of course I do," Pepper acknowledged, his eyes sparkling with the challenge. "But what can I do to help?"

"Well, you're the poet laureate around here," Tilley said with an appreciative smile. "I thought maybe you'd help us write the clues."

Pepper nodded eagerly. "Sure thing. I'd like that."

Tilley had known she could count on him, but she was pleased nevertheless by his quick response. "Of course, no one, absolutely no one, must know the answer. If

David had his way, only the two of us would know where the treasure is hidden. But I finally convinced him that if he didn't want to trust his advertising department to write the clues, he could certainly trust you. The sanctity of the confessional and all that," she teased, alluding to Pepper's joke about being a bartender. "And David trusts you. You have such a delightful way with words. Everything hinges on the clues, and I told David that I'd trust you with my life," she grinned, "though I'm sure that bit of melodrama wasn't really necessary."

Pepper laughed goodnaturedly. "Tell him I'll take a lie detector test."

"Oh, I don't think he'd go that far," she said hesitantly. Knowing David as well as she did already, Tilley thought that she'd better not make the suggestion.

Pepper eyed her thoughtfully. "I suppose the secrecy goes for everyone around here, too?" He seemed to be seriously considering the situation.

"Right," Tilley confirmed, reaching for her jacket and rising to leave. "Jacques and the twins will be good barometers of the public response. Their guesses should tell us how successful the clues are."

Pepper agreed, though he seemed to have some reservations. "Well, okay. I just thought it would be nice if I could tell Amelia. It might cheer her up."

Tilley sat back down. "You mean you found out what's wrong?" She watched as the dark-haired man reached for another box and got to work. "Don't pull that confidentiality stuff on me, Pepper. Give. I've got a right to know. I've been as worried about Amelia as anyone."

Pepper pushed the box aside and looked her right in

the eye. "She came by the bar for a beer the other night and finally started talking about it. It seems that Billy's thinking about leaving school for a career in the pro football league. Amelia doesn't know what to think, and she's climbing the walls about it. Now, to make matters worse, she's worried about her grades."

"What did you tell her?"

"Oh, nothing terribly helpful," Pepper said with a grimace. "I told her if it was true love, it would all work out. If not—if Billy loved football better than Amelia— then she was better off without him. She'll get over it. By the time she left, she was already talking about a new art project for her sculpture class. She'll come around." He nodded firmly. "I think it was a relief for her to talk about it. Now she may start pulling out of it, no matter what Billy decides to do."

"Pepper, you *are* good at your job," Tilley said with a sigh. "I don't see how you do it, but I'm glad you do."

Pepper went back to work, and Tilley noticed that he was blushing slightly. "Well, let's talk about this clue business," he said, changing the subject. "When do you need them?"

Tilley walked over to a wall calendar and began to study the dates. "The clues should start running every Sunday just as soon as possible. David's going to announce the hunt at the ball tonight, and he'll have the grand prize on display for the press."

"Grand prize?" Pepper echoed. "What's that going to be? I thought it would be the traditional golden egg."

"Well, it's that, but it's more than that," Tilley explained. She frowned. "David's being very mysterious

61

about it—he won't even tell me. But I'll find out tonight with everybody else and I'll let you know. Whatever it is, it's being donated by Danforth's."

Pepper whistled. "He's really putting his money where his mouth is, isn't he?"

Tilley nodded. "He says that if something is worth doing, it's worth doing in a big way. That's the way David does things."

"David?" Pepper's voice was teasing, but she couldn't see his face to make sure. "Sounds like you two are getting along pretty well."

Tilley reached for her jacket again, refusing to rise to the bait. "I suppose we are," she said finally, "for two people who're as different as can be. I'd better get going, Pepper. I'll talk to you about the clues tomorrow." She gave him a fond wave and headed out the door.

She shook her head slightly as she pulled the VW out on Kirby Drive and headed for River Oaks. Pepper had really hit on something, she mused. She and David were getting along, even though she had some doubts about him. He was handsome, he was charming, and he'd gotten involved with the Park People with what seemed to be total commitment. In her intervening meetings with him, Tilley had found him to be more than just an idea man. He was interesting and funny, and she found herself thinking back over the things he'd said about marriage. He was clearly a man who'd been hurt.

She couldn't help wondering what the Danforth mansion was like. She knew from local lore that it had been built by David's grandfather, who'd made his first fortune in cotton. The retail store was something he'd opened toward the latter part of his life, when he hoped to exchange the wheeling and dealing of his younger days for a less flamboyant way of life. Flamboyance was, however, a way of life for the elder Danforth, and the store was soon the most exclusive specialty shop in town. When David said that Danforth's specialized in treasures, he wasn't kidding.

She rounded a corner and headed down Chevy Chase. It didn't take Tilley long to figure out which of the fine homes was the Danforth residence because the circular drive in front was lined with expensive cars and beautifully attired guests were entering the house. For just a moment, she felt her heart skip a beat. She wouldn't know a soul there except David and a few of the Park People and what if—?

What if what? she asked herself sternly. It wasn't as if she'd never been to such a party, and after a full social life in New York City, there was little she hadn't seen or done. Still, this was something new, and she realized how really out of touch she was with this kind of event. Her own life was much quieter now and—she giggled softly to herself—was perhaps too quiet.

With an amused smile, she handed the keys to her VW to the parking valet and hurried up the front steps into the spacious entry hall, stopping briefly to admire the ornate chandelier that filled the doorway with brilliant light. The floor was black marble, and over to one side a staircase wound its way up to the second floor. There had been no one at the door so she slowly made her way through the throng of people, her usual poise and assurance returning with every step.

Standing at the arched doorway to the enormous living room, Tilley searched the crowd with her eyes. The walls of the long room were studded with rows of French windows on the front and French doors along the back, opening out to gardens in warmer months, Tilley surmised. At the far end of the room, a band was playing soft romantic melodies with a big band sound, and a large dance floor was filled with couples. The men wore tuxedos and ruffled shirts, and the women were in long dresses of every color imaginable. The sleek contemporary furniture had been moved to one end, and those guests who weren't dancing were conversing in groups of three and four. Circulating among the guests, a man and a woman dressed in black uniforms were passing silver trays of hors d'oeuvres and cocktails. What was she to do now? As ridiculous as she knew it was, she was rather hurt that David hadn't been waiting for her. He was the one who had insisted on her coming. It hadn't been her idea!

A moment later, a hand shot up from the far corner of the room, signaling her attention. It was David, and instinctively Tilley caught her breath. She never ceased to be astonished at how handsome he was. Everyone else in the room paled beside him, and she didn't doubt for a moment that in any crowd he would have merited such a distinction. He wore a single-breasted three-piece black tuxedo with a black silk bow tie, and his dark brown hair was neatly trimmed and carefully in place. His tall slim form was graceful in spite of his height, and there was an elegance about his every movement. He was now moving across the room toward her, and Tilley's pulse quickened as she headed in his direction.

"And she's beautiful as well," he said with an engaging grin. "As if making the best candy in the world weren't enough."

Tilley acknowledged his gallantry with a smile, then moved on to other subjects. "What a wonderful house!" she said with genuine enthusiasm.

"Yes, it is, isn't it?" David answered, though not as immodestly as his words would indicate. "But I get none of the credit. My grandfather built it, and a Danforth has lived here ever since." He looked around at the magnificent room. "Most of the time I forget how lovely it is and wonder at the insanity that keeps me living here all alone."

Tilley thought his remark was as disarming as his smile, and her heart softened a little. But before she had a chance to reply, the housekeeper was at her elbow, offering to take her jacket. David continued to talk.

"I'm sorry I wasn't there to meet you at the door, but I got hung up talking to someone about the park project. There are all kinds of people here who'll be interested, I'm sure. See? Linda's making the rounds right now." He and Tilley waved at the professor, who was holding court across the room. Tilley was glad to see her, glad to be reminded of the reason she was here. It wasn't merely a social event—she was here to accomplish something.

"Is this the candy maker you've been raving about? I'm almost surprised to see you here without a basket of chocolate eggs!" Tilley laughed as she accepted the outstretched hand of a tall distinguished gentleman with a red carnation in his lapel.

"The one and only," David said, stepping back slightly to include the newcomer. "Tilley, I want you to meet Simon Browning, the head of our marketing department. I've told him all about Parker Park and have enlisted his help with the Easter egg hunt."

"I'm pleased to meet you, Mr. Browning," Tilley said, firmly shaking his hand, "and I'll make sure you get all the Easter eggs you can possibly eat if you're helping the Park People."

"If they're as wonderful as David says they are, that should be quite a few," Simon returned courteously, and for the next several minutes, he and Tilley exchanged pleasantries about the upcoming event. Soon they were joined by still others who wanted to meet Tilley and to learn more about the Park People as well as the Chocolate Moose. She was gratified to hear how many of them had been in the store and liked it. It was forty-five minutes before she and David had another chance to talk alone, though he had never been far from her side. It was a nice feeling, she had to admit, to have him be so attentive, almost as if he were her date for the evening.

"And to think this is just the beginning," he finally whispered in her ear when there was a break in the conversation. "Didn't I tell you they'd be wild for you?"

"That's not exactly what you said," Tilley responded, remembering his reasonable approach. "You said we could make a lot of good contacts here. But I have to admit I'm flattered. It's nice to have so much attention. I just hope that all these people really do what they say they will to help Parker Park."

"Oh, they will," David assured her. "And then they'll be coming into the Chocolate Moose as regulars. Mark my words. If you won't let me sell your candy, I stand to lose a lot of money."

Tilley couldn't help but be amused by this whole-hearted, outrageous flattery. "Oh, I don't think you'll go broke," she teased, "and I told you we'd talk about that later."

"I'll hold you to it," he said firmly. "You can be sure of that." The challenge in his eyes belied the arrogance of his words. He looked around the room, fidgeting slightly with his black silk tie. He was studying the dancers. In the silence that followed, the enticing sound of the music could not be ignored. "Would you like to dance?" he asked, almost awkwardly.

Tilley was a little surprised at his unexpected lack of polish, though she wouldn't have acknowledged it for the world. "I'd love to," she answered simply, and almost immediately she found herself caught up in his arms, and he began to lead her skillfully around the dance floor.

Once they began to move, David seemed to relax, and his brown eyes never wavered as he looked down at Tilley. From the moment he put his arms around her, she was spellbound. Indeed, they both seemed to be, and Tilley no longer heard the voice of good sense warning her to be careful. They might have been the only couple in the room. She was secure in his arms, moved deeply by the music and the magnetism that tugged constantly at her. Words were not important as they shared a silence full of innuendo and intimacy. When the music stopped, it was a moment or two before they also paused, neither seeming to want to let go of the moment. When finally it was impossible to linger any longer, David released Tilley without letting go of her hand.

Looking down at her, he said, "I knew it would be like that with you—from the moment I first saw you." He reached out and gently touched her hair.

The gesture seemed quite natural to Tilley, but her own response was stilted. "Thank you," she said formally. Somehow she found herself holding back, being too careful, even when she wanted something else entirely. Quickly she begged off to go to the powder room, as much to hide her ambivalence as to powder her nose.

When she returned to the living room, David was preparing to make his announcement. He called her to his side, but this time he was once again the entrepreneur, the businessman.

"And now the moment you've all been waiting for," he began, with a trace of humor. He ran through the details of the Easter egg hunt, the rules, the procedures. Then he reached into his pocket and pulled out a small jeweler's box and held it up for all to see.

"The grand prize, ladies and gentlemen," he said with dramatic effect. Then turning to Tilley, he handed her the box. "You open it," he said, a hint of gentleness in his voice.

Meeting his eyes unflinchingly, she took the box from his hand. Dropping her gaze, she slowly opened the velvet case. She caught her breath. Inside was a beautiful gold egg, elaborately studded with precious jewels.

"It was made by Danforth's jewelers," David explained simply. And then as if it weren't obvious, he added, "It's real gold—and the gems are real as well."

Tilley looked up at him, her eyes wide with astonishment. "That should draw quite a crowd," she said quietly.

"Those are my intentions," David answered, a hard edge to his voice. "Local headlines to be sure, perhaps even some television coverage. It looks like you'll get a lot of attention for Parker Park, and it won't hurt Danforth's or the Chocolate Moose either."

Later, when most of the guests were leaving, David held Tilley back with one thing or another. He wouldn't let her leave. They lingered in the ballroom, saying goodnight to both old and new friends. It had truly been a magical evening, and she was sorry to see that the musicians were getting ready to pack up. David must have felt the same way. He went up to the piano player and said something, then walked back to Tilley and held out his arm. "I believe this is our dance, Ms. Hart," he said.

"So it is, Mr. Danforth," she replied, and she glided into his arms, the strains of "As Time Goes By" filling the room.

This time they covered the ballroom floor in a small circle, familiar partners now, each used to the nuances of the other's movements. David held Tilley close, and she drank in the smell of his cologne, the strength of the shoulder beneath her hand. She leaned toward him and put her head on his shoulder, not knowing, not caring what he might think. She thought he brushed her hair with his lips, but she couldn't be sure. She was so caught in the spell of the man and the music and the evening that she didn't care. When the music stopped, she drew back with a start, as if returning to her cold reality. "I could ask them to play on," David suggested, a question in his eyes.

But Tilley was already shocked at herself. "Oh, no, you mustn't do that," she said hurriedly. "I've really got to go."

"Are you sure?" he insisted. "I could dance all night."

"So could I," she said softly, "but we'd both regret it tomorrow." She broke out of his arms and headed for the door. David followed immediately and found her jacket and purse for her, holding the velvet jacket as she put it on.

"Do you ever do anything in a small way?" Tilley couldn't resist asking as David told the valet to fetch her car.

"Not if I can help it," was the smooth reply. He turned to face her.

"And do you always get what you want?" She was rambling and she knew it. They were alone on the wide porch, a man and a woman together under the moonlight.

"Always," he said without hesitation, his brown eyes enigmatic as he searched her face. "Happy Valentine's Day, Tilley."

Suddenly he gathered her in his arms, his lips pressed against her own. She had known this moment was approaching, for they had been leading up to it all evening, but what surprised her was her own swift reaction to the embrace, the wave of desire which shook her, the sensual onslaught that made her knees weak, her heart pound faster. Almost as quickly as he had captured her, David released his hold. She could see her car coming up the driveway.

"One way or another." His final words before she got into the car were gruff, almost a threat.

4

Oh no, I was afraid this would happen!'' Tilley exclaimed, a frown of dismay creasing her forehead as she studied the note she held in her hand. Somehow she'd lost an entire month. How had she ever gotten so behind? She'd been working ten or twelve hours a day, seven days a week, and it still seemed like she'd never catch up. This note was positive proof.

She sank down at her desk, still wearing her soft wool jacket. Though spring was right around the corner, there was still a hint of coolness in the air, and Tilley had chosen a kelly green shirt to wear with her crisp jeans. Jacques came in and found her there, still looking at the note.

"What's the matter?" he asked with concern. "You

haven't even taken off your coat. Is that a note from Pepper?"

"Right," Tilley affirmed unhappily as she shrugged out of her jacket. "We've got a problem—and it's all my fault. I've almost got the copy for the new catalog in shape, but I've been putting it off while we've all been trying to get ready for the Easter egg hunt. Now Pepper says we're literally down to the last one. I've got to finish it today and get it to the printer. That's all there is to it."

"Then that's what you'll do," Jacques declared firmly. "Rachel and I can take care of the customers while you work on it, and Amelia is coming later to work on the candy for the Easter egg hunt." It took a lot to upset Jacques, and this clearly wasn't enough. He took the situation completely in stride.

"We'll what?" Rachel demanded as she arrived, taking off her backpack and bicycle clips. "What's Jacques volunteering me for now?" She gave them both a broad smile to let them know she wasn't really worried.

Tilley quickly appraised her of the situation and concluded, "It's all my fault, really. If I hadn't gotten so involved with the Park People, we wouldn't be this behind. But if you could give me as much free time as you can today, I think I can catch up. And send Amelia in to see me when she gets here."

"No problem." Rachel went to unlock the front door and put change in the cash register for the day, while Jacques went to work in the kitchen.

Tilley poked through her files until she found the catalog copy she'd already completed. There wasn't as much to do as she had thought, so she began to relax a little. Then she reached for her address book to look up the number of Sam Vernon's print shop and tried to think when she could reasonably deliver the camera-ready copy. Maybe she'd better plan on tomorrow morning to give herself some leeway.

No sooner had she put her hand on the receiver than the phone rang, the jarring sound catching her off guard.

"The Chocolate Moose!" she said with more enthusiasm than she actually felt. "Good morning."

"Good morning to you," was the cheerful reply. By now, that deep masculine voice was very familiar to her. "Am I catching you at a bad time?"

"No, why?" Tilley had thought that she'd sounded cheerful enough, though she was beginning to understand that it was hard to hide anything from David. Among other things, he seemed to assess people's moods pretty shrewdly.

"Oh, you just sounded a little breathless, that's all," he replied evenly.

Tilley relaxed a little. "Well, I was just reaching for the phone when it rang. It surprised me." She knew she was deliberately trying to sound cheerful. She didn't like to think about the strong feelings that even hearing David's voice could arouse in her. She remembered all too well that embrace after the Valentine's Day ball, for it had shaken her to her very depths.

His next remark was openly flirtatious. "I guess it would be too much to hope for to think you were about to call me, wouldn't it? I couldn't be that lucky."

"As a matter of fact, I wasn't," Tilley said lightly. "I was about to call an absolutely wonderful man named Sam Vernon, though." She waited for his reaction, but it wasn't at all what she expected.

"Sam Vernon?" David asked with interest. "I know him! He prints our catalog. What are you working on, Tilley?"

She almost groaned right into the receiver. Sometimes it seemed as if Houston was just a small town—everyone knew everyone else. "He's my printer, too," she admitted. "I've gotten a little bit behind over here, thanks to you, and I'm running out of mail order catalogs."

"Thanks to me?" David asked. "I don't understand."

"I was only joking," she explained. "It's just that I've been working so hard on the Easter egg hunt that I've neglected the Chocolate Moose a bit. And we've been deluged with requests for catalogs. Pepper's frantic, trying to answer all the mail."

"That article in the gourmet magazine must have reached a lot of people," David suggested.

"Sure looks that way," Tilley agreed. "And the publicity for the Easter egg hunt so far has been an added boost. Now we're down to our very last catalog and I've got to get the new layout to Sam just as soon as I can. So you can see I've got my hands full."

"Then I'll help," David said decisively. "I was going to ask you out to dinner tonight. That's the reason I called."

"Thanks, but no thanks," Tilley replied, her heart beating a little faster. "I've got all I can handle at the moment."

David wasn't going to give her a moment's reprieve.

"All the more reason to let me help. I'll even bring dinner. How about Renu's chicken with basil? I'll get takeout and be over around seven thirty. How much has to be done?"

"Well," Tilley answered thoughtfully, choosing to ignore his plans for dinner. "I'd like to use the same layout, but there are a lot of things I'd like to change as long as I'm doing it anyway. I want to write new copy for the entire catalog, spice it up a bit. And we've got a few candies to add. It's not really that much, but I've got to do it, and do it fast."

"Well, if that's all you're worried about, your problems are over," David said airily. "I'm not only offering to feed you, but I'll be bringing the talents of the best catalog man in the business to boot—that's me."

Tilley bristled slightly at the insinuation. "I know a thing or two about this myself. You're not the only one with experience."

There was a note of apology in his voice when he spoke again. "I know that, Tilley. Don't be so sensitive. It'll be more fun if we do it together. I'm only offering to help."

Perhaps he was right. Her nerves were a bit raw this morning. "That may be—"

"No maybe about it." And it was clear from David's tone of voice that he wouldn't take no for an answer. "I'll be over at seven thirty sharp, pencil in hand. See you then." He hung up the phone.

Oh, dear, she thought, here he comes again—the human whirlwind. She remembered how he'd taken over the first meeting of the Park People and wondered what she'd let herself in for. But she also knew that they worked well together, and she had to be honest with herself: she wanted to see him again. If there was a reason for it, so much the better. Despite all her sensible warnings about getting too involved with the man, she knew she was looking forward to the evening. Tilley was glad he hadn't let her say no. She had the feeling that their relationship was taking a new turn, and she wanted to see where it would all lead.

"Tilley?" Amelia paused in the doorway, a puzzled look on her face. "Jacques said you wanted to talk to me. What about? I'm doing a lot better. I really am."

Tilley was touched by her remark. At least Amelia knew that they were all concerned about her. "Yes, Amelia," she said with a smile. "I do want to talk, but not about anything personal. That's your business," she said, noticing Amelia's sigh of relief. The girl sank down into one of the chairs opposite Tilley's desk. "What I have to say is not about that at all." Tilley paused and looked through the papers she had in her hand, then passed them across to Amelia.

"What are these?" she asked. "They look like recipes. Oh, I know—this is the stuff for the cookbook. Oh, Tilley, you've gotten a lot done. Do you want me to read them, or check them, or what?"

"You don't need to read them, really," Tilley said with a grin. "You probably know them all by heart. And I thought Jacques and I would do the checking. No, I want you to do something else entirely." She paused, then concluded triumphantly, "I want you to illustrate the cookbook."

Amelia's eyes widened in surprise. "Me? But Tilley, I'm sure your publisher could get you anybody you wanted."

"That's right," Tilley affirmed. "And I want you. Who better? You know the Chocolate Moose, you love the store, and I know you'd do your very best. Just take these and see what you can come up with. I have perfect confidence in you. I've seen your art projects. I even like the doodles you leave on notepads around here. My editor and I are working on a contract for you right now. She wants to see some preliminary sketches and talk to you about the format."

Amelia seemed genuinely stunned, but when she raised her eyes to Tilley, they were shining with excitement. "A book! I get to illustrate a book! Oh, Tilley, you really think I can do it?"

"I know you can," Tilley grinned, pleased at Amelia's reaction. "So get to it!"

"I will, I will," Amelia promised. "But now I'd better get back to work. The phone keeps ringing off the wall with questions about the Easter egg hunt, and it's about time for Rachel to take a break." She put the recipes in her backpack in the closet and went out humming.

"That was a very nice thing you did, Tilley," Jacques said in an approving tone when she went into the kitchen.

"It wasn't nice at all, Jacques," Tilley demurred as she took a tray of candy across to a table and began to decorate it. "It was smart. Amelia will do a wonderful job.

If it happens to make her feel better, then that's lucky all around."

"Hmmph!" Jacques obviously didn't believe her.

The rest of the day flew by, though Tilley didn't get as much done on the catalog as she'd hoped. Sam Vernon had assured her that he'd save some press time for the catalogs, and she'd promised faithfully to have the copy there the next morning. Then in the morning mail, a new shipment of unsweetened chocolate arrived that she'd ordered directly from Germany, and she spent some time in the kitchen checking it out. She and Jacques declared that it was better than they'd had a right to expect.

That afternoon, Jacques had insisted that she taste the lemon divinity, a confection they hoped to add to their spring repertoire. He hadn't made any divinity in years, or so he said, and it was a favorite recipe of Tilley's. Caught up in the process, she spent most of the afternoon with Jacques mixing up several batches of pale yellow candy until both of them were satisfied with the results. When Amelia came in to say she was locking up for the day, Tilley couldn't have been more surprised.

Brushing a stray curl out of her face with the back of her hand, Tilley said, "It can't be that time already!" She looked at the clock with dismay, but it only confirmed her worst suspicions.

"How time flies when you're having fun!" Amelia teased, then she turned to Tilley with a serious expression. "And I want to let you know that I'll have some sketches for the cookbook ready soon. I'm looking forward to it."

"I can't wait," Tilley said with forced heartiness. She'd almost forgotten about it already—still another project she had to complete. "How were sales this afternoon?"

"Couldn't be better," Amelia reported. "We may even need another part-time clerk soon, if business keeps up at this rate."

"That's good to hear," Tilley said absently, her mind racing on to the next task. "Is the bank deposit ready?"

"You bet," Amelia answered. "And everything's locked up for the night. I'm on my way."

"Thanks," Tilley said gratefully. "We'll be right behind you. Jacques is almost through with the dishes, and I've got to get to work. If I don't get that layout to Sam tomorrow, we're going to have to eat this candy ourselves." She waited until they'd both left and locked up behind them, noting that she still had an hour to shower and change.

But when she reached the apartment, she impulsively decided to set the table for dinner. She opened up the small gateleg table that had been her grandmother's and set out her good china and silver. Something in her wanted to make this a special occasion, and she wondered briefly at her own high spirits, especially when she knew she had so much work to do. What was it about David that made her feel this way? But she headed off to the shower, determined not to think about it. No time for daydreaming, she admonished herself.

Thirty minutes later, she hurried back downstairs to start working on the layout again. She had changed to jeans and penny loafers and a pale green cashmere sweater, its short sleeves and scooped neck a perfect foil for her coloring. Her hair was freshly washed and pulled back with mother-of-pearl combs, and she smelled faintly of a new perfume.

When the front doorbell rang, she was completely engrossed in her work, her face flushed with intense concentration. When she answered the door, she was oblivious to her beauty, her cheeks rosy, her brown eyes bright, her smile radiant.

"Hello," she said as she opened the door, delighted to see David. She stuck a pencil behind her ear, as she reached out to help him with his burdens.

"Dinner as promised," David announced, surrendering some of the carry-out sacks from Renu's, the local Thai restaurant. He paused, looking her over with pleasure. "I have to tell you," he said with mock seriousness, "that it just won't do to have you opening the door looking like that. It can't possibly be good for business. How can anyone concentrate on candy with you in the same room?"

Tilley blushed slightly and waited for him to come in so she could lock the door. "You forget what good candy I make. It's hard to compete with something that good." She sniffed hungrily at the boxes. "But this might just do it." She looked up into his eyes and smiled.

David walked into the kitchen, and Tilley locked up and followed him. "What's first on the agenda—work or dinner?" He seemed agreeable enough.

"I don't know about you, but I'm starving," she admitted frankly. "Come on, we'll eat at my place." She didn't acknowledge his surprised expression but headed for the stairs.

David was right behind her. "You know, you told me you lived above the store, but it's hard for me to imagine. I think I've always imagined you sleeping next to the stove in the kitchen or something—like an elf. You really have a regular place?"

"As you can see, I do," Tilley said, opening the front door. She led him into the small living room. Over by the window, the elegantly set table was particularly inviting, and she was pleased with the results of her efforts.

"What a wonderful place to live," David said, looking around the room with interest, the light in his eyes genuinely enthusiastic. "It feels just the way a home is supposed to feel."

Tilley watched as he walked over to the bookcases and ran his fingers over the row of books. "Thank you," she said softly, somehow touched by his initial response. Then she continued with her usual frankness, "I believe you really mean that."

David turned to her, looking slightly affronted. "Of course, I do," he said. "I can't help but compare this to the mausoleum I live in. I don't even know for sure how many rooms are in that house!"

Tilley set the cartons of food down on the table. "Oh, come on," she said skeptically.

David made a wry face. "Maybe I'm exaggerating a little," he admitted as he carried the sack of beer into the small kitchen. "Hey, where's the bottle opener?"

Tilley could hear him opening and closing cabinet drawers. "In the drawer next to the sink."

"Aha!" he exclaimed, obviously finding what he wanted. Then, as he came back into the living room, he said, "I dream of living in a cozy little apartment just like this one."

Tilley lit the candles on the table. "Then why don't you?"

David walked to the table and set down the open bottles of beer. "It's a long story." He was standing beside her now, very close. He took the burning match from her hand, then bent to brush her lips gently before blowing out the flame.

Tilley was taken aback by the intimacy of the gesture, but she did her best not to act as if anything out of the ordinary had occurred. "I'm in no hurry," she replied, taking a seat. "That is, if we can talk and eat at the same time. I'm afraid I'm not a very good listener when I'm hungry."

David sat down across from her and took the spring roll she offered him. "Dig in! I'd hate to stand in the way of a healthy appetite."

She laughed as she spooned the delicious chicken onto plates for both of them. "Don't worry about that, nothing interferes with my appetite. But you're changing the subject. We were talking about your house, remember?"

"Technically, the house isn't mine." He paused, taking a bite. "It's my father's and he doesn't want to sell it. He's been living quite happily in London for the past ten years, and as far as I know, he has no intention of coming back to Houston. But he wants a place to come home to if he does. An ace in the hole is the expression, I believe."

"A place where, when you go, they have to take you in?" Tilley asked, meeting his eyes directly.

"That's it exactly," David concurred with a sigh.

"But that still doesn't explain why you live there alone," Tilley insisted, pouring the beer into glasses, watching carefully to see that the foam didn't spill over.

"Oh, it's hard to change," David admitted with a shrug. "I can't see the expense of keeping up two households. I couldn't lock up that house and let it go to ruin." He was silent for a moment while he ate, obviously thinking about his next words. "And it is the family home. Who knows? Maybe I'll have a family there someday. The pitter-patter of little feet—that's all that house needs." He chuckled to himself.

Tilley was surprised. "Hey, you'd better watch out. You could ruin your reputation with talk like that," she teased, dodging the real issue of marriage and families.

"That might not be so bad," he returned with a mysterious smile. Tilley felt a little shiver of apprehension. Was he trying to tell her something? She felt sorry that her flippant remark had probably forestalled any further confidence.

David went on. "I'm sure I can trust you not to tell the world that David Danforth has a tender streak. Not that anyone would believe you, of course."

Tilley laughed halfheartedly, the closeness of the moment gone. What was there about this man that caused her to back off, to run for cover at the slightest hint of intimacy? But even as they continued to talk about other things as they finished their supper, she knew the answer to the question, knew it as well as anyone knows her own heart. She was dangerously close to letting herself fall in love with him. Every time he looked at her, she felt a clamor of emotions, almost as if he had touched her with his hand, run his fingers over her innermost feelings. Tilley felt as though she were succumbing to his charms, his lighthearted manner, his endearing gestures.

When they were finished, they carried their dishes to the kitchen, opened two more beers and hurried downstairs to work on the layouts.

As they worked side by side in the studio, Tilley realized that the closeness between them had been transformed into a kind of tension, its hold on them not loosened but changed into something powerful and electrifying. She was constantly aware of how alone they were, and she was relieved when David stuck steadfastly to the business at hand.

"You know, I could save you a lot of trouble with this," he commented drily.

Tilley had the distinct feeling that she knew what was coming next. "How's that?"

"If you'd just give Danforth's exclusive rights as your distributor, we could make short work of all this, take care of the catalog, fill the orders out of our shipping department. It would be easy." He gently laid a page he had just pasted up to one side and looked at her.

"Thanks, but I like the way it works right now," she returned. "The only reason I'm caught a little short at the moment is that I've taken on so much with the Easter egg hunt. Most of the time, the mail order business pretty much runs itself. But if I change my mind, I'll let you know," she added with a smile.

"I'm serious about this," David insisted. "If you'd let me, I could sell your candy out the door in no time."

"I'm sure you could," she said matter-of-factly, "but I'm afraid that would take a lot of expansion. I came back to Houston to run a small business and to run it my way. And that's exactly what I'm doing, thank you very much."

"And doing it very well," David said, helping himself to a second piece of lemon divinity. "But like I said, I'll be ready if and when you change your mind."

It wasn't that she would mind selling her candy at Danforth's, Tilley reflected, it was just that she wasn't ready to give up distribution rights. Maybe she should think about it a little more. "Let's talk about this again," she said lightly. "Maybe we can work something out."

"Now *that* I can live with," David said with a grin. "Here, what do you think of this?" He handed her another page, and she exchanged it for the one she had just finished working on.

"Looks fabulous," she said, perusing it carefully. Tilley had been pleased with David's suggestions. His eye for design was keen and original, and his skill with the technical details was impressive. He knew the ropes from practical experience, and she couldn't help but be grateful that he was taking the time to help her.

"That about does it," she said with satisfaction, putting all the pages in a folder and placing it on her desk. "You know, I owe you an apology," she continued, turning to face him. "You're good, very good." Despite the late hour, she felt as fresh as she had when they'd started.

Their work had been so rewarding, so special, that she felt energized.

David arched an eyebrow. "You sound surprised! Running a family business isn't necessarily synonymous with being a dilettante, you know."

His answer seemed rehearsed, and Tilley guessed she had made the obvious assumption, one that he had heard often. She nodded. "I suppose I thought Danforth's was your silver spoon. I didn't take into account how hard you must have worked at it."

He grinned hopefully. "Maybe tonight's the night for dispelling myths and ruining reputations. Thanks for the compliment. I've spent a lifetime trying to prove that I'm a perfectly good businessman in my own right. Living down a silver spoon isn't easy." He was leaning against a drawing board. The light fell on his face in shadows, and there was an earnest quality in his voice.

"I'm sure," Tilley said, equally serious.

"There's another myth I'd like to dispel tonight," he continued, his voice soft and seductive.

This time, Tilley knew better than to be flippant. She was seeing a part of this man that she liked, a side she hadn't expected. This allowed her to acknowledge the less sensible cries of her heart. And she didn't move when he came over to stand in front of her, very close. The last thing she wanted was to push him away. "What's that?" she asked, her voice almost a whisper.

"You know what I'm talking about," he reminded her gently. "You've been teasing me about it all evening."

Tilley felt a powerful pull, as if he were willing her to his arms. "You mean your reputation as a ladies' man?" she asked, trying to sound lighthearted.

"I'm not, you know," he said, his hands spanning her waist, drawing her close. "I'm really not."

"I think I know that," Tilley said, looking up at him. Her eyes sought the curve of his mouth, and she knew he was about to kiss her. She offered no protest, ready for the inevitable, more than willing. If anything, she was relieved that the tension had finally been broken, that the attraction between them had truly been acknowledged. As his lips pressed against hers, she was only surprised at how right she felt, how swiftly she responded to his embrace.

He released her lips but held her close, his brown eyes searching for something more. "I've never known a woman like you, Tilley. You make me want to be more than I am. It's almost as though you expect it of me." There was a puzzled look on his handsome face, as if he were wrestling with a demon of his own.

"That's funny," Tilley admitted honestly, "And all this time I though *you* were pushing me." She put her arms around his neck, feeling secure somehow, secure and aroused. Could it be that they were no longer playing games with each other? "Sometimes you frighten me, you press so hard."

A flicker of pain crossed David's face. "That's the last thing I want—to frighten you." He looked into her eyes and saw his own hunger reflected in her brown ones. Without another word, he kissed her again, this time with more force, more determination. Tilley gave her self up to the moment, and when his tongue parted her lips and sought out the velvet interior of her mouth, she tightened her hold on him, her fingers caught in the dark tangle of hair at his neck.

He reached down to cup her hips, pulling her close, and Tilley arched her body against his with a sudden awareness of his need for her. He pressed her to him hungrily, and she was past caring what happened when they both heard a key turn in the front lock.

They broke apart suddenly as Pepper's voice echoed through the kitchen. "Tilley, are you here?" They moved to the doorway as the sound of his footsteps crossed the kitchen toward them.

"Hi, Pepper," she said brightly, trying not to feel embarrassed. David stood beside her, giving Pepper a welcoming smile.

"How are you doing?" Pepper asked cheerily.

"Oh, working on the new catalog," Tilley replied. "Come on in, take a look."

"Have a beer," David offered, going upstairs to fetch one. Tilley was grateful for his quick recovery from the awkward moment and pleased to see him make himself at home.

The three of them spent a pleasant half-hour discussing the catalog, until Pepper finally said, "Okay, you two. I've got to get to work. I see a stack of orders, and I'd better start packing up chocolate moose or I'll be here all night."

They said good night to Pepper, then Tilley walked

David to the front of the store and stood there for a moment, not sure what to say. David leaned down and brushed her lips gently. "You'd better get some sleep," he said softly.

"Sometimes it's like Grand Central Station around here," Tilley began apologetically, but David stopped her with a finger over her lips.

"To be continued," he promised. "After all," he said lightly, "you know the old maxim, 'If you can't stand the heat, stay out of the kitchen.' This is one kitchen I like. Next time we won't be interrupted, I can promise you that." He opened the door Tilley had regretfully unlocked for him and walked out into the night, throwing her a kiss.

5

Tilley peeked out her second-story window, anxiously checking the weather: it was clear and sunny just as the forecast had promised. She had a hard time believing that Easter—and spring with it—had actually arrived. The last weeks she'd hardly taken a step out of the store, and she was looking forward to the Easter egg hunt today, if only for the chance at having some well-deserved, long-awaited fun. Don't kid yourself, girl, she admonished herself, you're looking forward to seeing David again. It's been a long time, too long, she thought, as she remembered that night they'd worked together on the catalog.

She threw on the clothes she had so carefully laid out the night before. The pale green linen skirt was one of her favorites, and the simple raspberry cotton sweater looked good with her hair. As an afterthought, she reached up to the top shelf of her closet and pulled down a large natural straw picture hat. Tying a pale green ribbon around its brim, she thought her outfit complete. Right down to the Easter bonnet, she laughed to herself. She wanted to look her best for this occasion.

Hurrying down to the kitchen, she looked for David's Easter present. Late the night before, she had come down and put it together, just for fun. It was a special Easter basket filled with bright green artificial grass, chocolate bunnies of all different sizes, and delicately painted eggs of sugary fondant. It seemed to her that this would be a nice way, a personal way, of letting David know how much she valued his work on the Easter egg hunt. Never hurts to spread a little good will, she told herself as she locked the door behind her and headed out toward her bright orange VW. Then she stopped. Who are you kidding, Tilley Hart? she asked herself sharply. This isn't just good will. You're looking for a way to tell David Danforth you think he's special. And that was the whole truth, the long and short of it.

She enjoyed the short drive out to the park, the warm spring air filling the small car like perfume. It was going to be a perfect day, she could tell. When she pulled up in front of Astroworld, she wasn't surprised to see David pacing in front of the gates of the amusement park, waiting for her. He looked wonderful in an ice cream suit of white cotton with a pale blue shirt and blue and white striped tie. She hurried toward him, the basket in her hands.

"Happy Easter!" she said brightly, handing it over. "I though that if you weren't going to hunt for candy like everyone else, that you should at least have some of your own."

David looked down at her elegant creation in surprise and smiled affectionately. "Thank you, Tilley. It's been a long time since anyone did anything like this for me."

"Then that's too long," she said easily. "Everyone needs something special now and then." She looked toward the interior of the park, trying to change the subject so she could avoid the tension that hung in the air between them. "Is everything all ready?"

"Ready as it'll ever be," David assured her. "All we need now are some kids to fill the place up."

"I doubt that there'll be any problem with that. I thought you said that the phones were ringing off the hook at Danforth's," she reminded him. "It's time to think big, David. Remember your motto," she teased. Despite her cheerful words, she felt a twinge of anticipation at how much was riding on this event. Parker Park might be saved or lost, depending on its outcome. Surely they would make enough money. David couldn't be wrong about this. They'd worked too hard and too long for it to fail.

"Oh, I am," David assured her. "I tend to get stage fright at the last minute sometimes." She was touched by his admission and was trying to think of an appropriate response when she saw Pepper, Amelia, and Rachel coming up the sidewalk.

"Happy Easter!" she called, and the group exchanged

greetings for a few moments until Pepper spoke up.

"Hey, David, who won the grand prize? Who solved all those wonderful clues that I wrote?"

David reached into his pocket and pulled out a slip of paper. "Someone named Genevieve Casey. I don't know who she is or anything else about her, but I'm sure she'll be here. And do you know hers was the only right answer?" He shook his head as if he couldn't believe it.

Pepper's expression was a little apologetic. "I didn't think the clues were that hard."

"Oh, they weren't," Rachel assured him airily. "I know exactly where the treasure is hidden." Everyone looked at her in complete amazement.

"Okay, where is it?" Amelia demanded, and everyone echoed her request. "Yeah, come on Rachel, where's the treasure?"

"Under the last seat of the rollercoaster—what do they call it?—the Texas Cyclone!" Rachel announced triumphantly. "It wasn't that hard."

"But how did you guess?" Tilley was curious, looking over at Pepper to see if he'd inadvertently let the cat out of the bag. He shook his head.

"It was easy," Rachel continued. "The clues were logical. I'm a computer science major. I take courses in logic for fun. It was just a matter of successful deductive thinking," she concluded, looking for all the world like a victorious Sherlock Holmes.

"Well, Rachel, I'm sorry you couldn't enter the contest," David said apologetically. "I'll have to think of an appropriate consolation prize. I know. You finish up that degree of yours and come see me about a job. Danforth's can always use a computer whiz."

"I'll do that," Rachel said seriously. "I'll be seeing you about it before you know it."

Their discussion was broken up as children of all ages began to arrive at Astroworld. Some came in groups, still others came with their parents, and Tilley was delighted to see that there seemed to be a lot of them. It was all going to work out after all. She was glad that they had a winner for the treasure, for that was the perfect finishing touch.

An hour later, the park was filled to the brim with excited children racing here and there, exclaiming with delight as they uncovered first one hidden egg, then another. Pretty soon people were wandering all over, comparing their finds, passing on hints of good places to look, and screaming with delight as they rode the rides that had been opened especially for them.

Danforth's employees had joined forces with the staff at the park to make sure that everyone had a good time, and Tilley noticed with satisfaction that all of her employees, even Sybil and Jacques, had turned out to help. For a moment, she felt as if she were surrounded by a single happy family. Every now and then, she and David would exchange pleased looks as they saw what a good time everyone was having, and Tilley noticed that he never got very far away from her, no matter where she went.

The Park People were all working hard, too. Linda Baker took Tilley aside for a moment. "We've never gotten this sort of public response to anything we've done. If this is the way you're starting off your term as president of the Park People, Tilley, then we're in really good shape."

"Now, now." Tilley didn't want to take all the credit. "I don't think this would have worked at all if it weren't for David. It was his idea in the first place."

"Well, *you* made all the candy," Linda pointed out. "Can't have an Easter egg hunt without candy." But she hurried off to thank David as well.

Tilley felt a surge of gratitude as she saw that dark handsome head across from her. He had been wonderful and patient all day long. She went over to talk to him herself. "I think this is a success," she told him. "And I thought yesterday was going to be one of the busiest days of the year!" She had spent all afternoon talking with people and enjoying their company, but it seemed that this Easter weekend had gone on forever!

"You don't know the half of it," David said mysteriously. He extracted himself from a group of children clamoring for his attention and came to her side, taking her hand. "Ready to call it a day? I told the Astroworld officials that they could close down in about an hour. Maybe we ought to announce the winner of the grand prize and start winding things down a bit. What do you think?"

"Seems like a good idea to me," Tilley replied. "The kids must be close to exhaustion by now. And some of the staff told me that there are parents lined up in cars outside waiting for their kids. As much fun as this is, it can't go on forever."

"That's right," David said regretfully, "though it

seems a shame. Everyone is having such a good time. Don't you remember when you were their age, Tilly? I remember wishing the good times would just go on and on forever."

As she walked with him to the central plaza to make the announcement, she felt close to David, and she sensed somehow that he had opened up to her in a way that was unusual for him. Clearly he was talking about more than the Easter egg hunt. Or did she only imagine that?

Suddenly David's voice crackled out from loudspeakers all over the park. "Please meet at the central plaza," he announced. "We'll be awarding the grand prize in a few minutes." There was a sudden scurry as children and their parents rushed around finding each other and made their way to the central plaza, the very heart of the park.

Tilley was standing next to David on the temporary stage that had been erected just for this moment. David was holding the microphone, and Tilley, uncomfortably aware of people's eyes on her, smiled pleasantly, trying to maintain her poise. She had known that this moment was inevitable, but she was so accustomed to keeping a low profile that she'd tried not to think about it. Public appearances just weren't her favorite part of being in business, but David seemed to thrive on it, and she smiled, remembering his earlier confession of stage fright. He was bending down at the edge of the stage, talking to several children and their parents, looking for all the world as if he did this every day. She was both glad and sorry that this project they had both worked so hard and so long on would soon be over.

He took her hand and pulled her to center stage next to him. "Ladies and gentlemen, boys and girls," he announced, drawing the hushed attention of the crowd. "I'd like you to meet the lady whose company made all those lovely Easter eggs you all are munching on. This is Tilley Hart, owner of the Chocolate Moose Candy Company and president of the Park People." The applause was deafening.

Tilley nodded her thanks as David went on.

"And now we'd like to announce the winner of our grand prize. This person must have read all the clues published in the newspaper very carefully in order to guess where the treasure was hidden. I think most of you will be surprised to know that only one person correctly guessed the answer. And the winner is—" He produced an envelope from the inside pocket of his jacket and held it out to Tilley, along with the microphone.

"And the winner is—" Tilley had caught the spirit of the moment and wanted to prolong the suspense as much as possible. "The winner is Genevieve Casey!"

The crowd broke into yells of surprise and applause as a small blond girl gingerly made her way toward the stage, blushing furiously at all the attention. "I never really thought I'd win," she whispered as Tilley bent down to give her a kiss on the cheek.

"But you did!" Tilley responded enthusiastically, trying to put the girl at ease. "You should be very proud of yourself."

David came over and took Genevieve's hand, leading her to the edge of the stage. "All right, Genevieve, now tell everyone where the treasure was hidden."

It was a good thing that David had the microphone, or the girl's reply would have scarcely been audible. "Under the last seat of the Texas Cyclone!"

There were groans of disappointment from people who had tried and failed to guess the answer. The adults in the audience laughed appreciatively, and Tilley knew that many of them were feeling regret at having overlooked the obvious and being outdone by a child. David once again took control of the moment. "Now for the treasure!" he said, reaching into his pockets as if pretending to look for something. "Ah, here it is!" he exclaimed, withdrawing a still-closed hand. He held his hand aloft, then slowly opened it, so everyone could see what he was holding. The golden egg caught the sun and sparkled brightly, and there were gasps of admiration on every side.

Genevieve looked as if she couldn't believe her eyes. "It's a real golden egg," she whispered.

"That's right," David assured her, handing it over. "Now look inside."

Genevieve very carefully looked the egg over, checking to see where it opened. Gently, she pulled the two halves of the egg apart. "It's a ring," she said breathlessly, "a ruby ring."

"That's exactly what it is," David said with a grin. "And though it looks a little big right now, I'm sure we can get it sized to fit your finger." He gave the girl an indulgent smile and turned back to face the crowd.

"Thank you for joining us at this very special Easter egg hunt. It was special not only because we had wonderful candy"—he smiled at Tilley—"and not only because Genevieve won a contest, but because so many of you came out here and spent your money for a good cause. I want to tell you that because there are so many of you out there, Houston will soon have another park—Parker Park in Montrose." He looked over to see Tilley's ecstatic reaction and then continued speaking. "Without all of your participation today, that would never have been possible. Thank you. The Park People, the Chocolate Moose, and Danforth's hope we can do this again next year and that you'll all be back—maybe in Parker Park." The crowd, satisfied that the big moment was over, applauded and began to drift away toward the nearest entrance.

It was over, and it had been a complete success. Tilley could scarcely believe it. When David had announced that they'd raised enough money for the park, she had felt a thrill of accomplishment, followed by a moment of utter disbelief. Had it really gone that well? But now the reporters were clustering around, and she knew it must be true. Still, having worked so long and so hard for that very moment, she was reluctant to let go of it. Her emotions were a complicated tangle of joy, relief, and regret.

Tilley knew that a portion of her regret stemmed from the fact that she no longer had a reason to be working with David. Looking at his dark head bent down close to Genevieve's face, she felt a surge of affection. All of her doubts about his motives for working with the Park People had vanished. He was the real thing, through and through.

Later, as the two of them walked hand in hand through

the gates of the park, David asked, "Sorry that it's over? I think there's always a letdown after something like this, even when it goes as well as this one did."

"You're right," Tilley admitted with a sigh. "I am going to miss all the excitement. What about you? Any regrets?"

"Not one," David said firmly. "I'm glad I had a chance to help. I wouldn't have missed a minute of it, Tilley."

They walked along in companionable silence, but Tilley knew that she wanted to say something more. "I've enjoyed working with you," she confided impulsively. "I'm going to miss that, too."

David raised his eyebrows quizzically. "I'm not going anywhere, Tilley. And I'm not letting you go just yet. I think we deserve a celebration."

Her heart leapt with sudden joy. "A celebration? Who did you have in mind?" Her mind was racing, and she was sorry that so many of the people who had worked on the project had already gone home. "I could call—"

David stopped her, turned to face her, and placed a finger over her lips to stop the flow of talk. "Sometimes it pays to think small, Tilley," he said quietly. "Say, in terms of two. You and me. What do you say?"

Tilley smiled with pleasure, for there wasn't a thing in the world she'd rather do. "I like you when you think small, David Danforth. I like it very much indeed. I say yes." She paused for a moment, then rushed on. "I'll fix dinner. Want to follow me over to my place?" At his hesitation, she said, "You brought the chicken and basil last time, remember? It's my turn."

David gave her a broad grin. "You're on. Meet you there in a few minutes." And bending down to brush her lips with his, he turned and walked to his car.

Tilley smiled to herself and got into her car, driving home quickly, her mind racing a mile a minute. What could they have for dinner? She thought she had a few steaks in the freezer, and she could thaw them in the microwave. She always had fresh vegetables for a salad, and there were potatoes to bake. If she recollected correctly, there might even be a bottle of wine someone had given her for Christmas in a cupboard somewhere.

When she got home, she left the back door open for David and hurried into the kitchen. The steaks looked beautiful, and she popped them into the microwave to thaw and hurried out to her tiny terrace to light charcoal in the hibachi. She had just gotten the fire started when she heard David's footsteps on the stairs.

"Happy Easter yourself!" he said, handing her a bouquet of spring flowers. "I'm not the only one who needs something special every now and then."

Tilley buried her nose in the flowers, inhaling the fragrance of carnations, roses, and daffodils. "Thank you," she said softly. "They're lovely." She turned to look for a vase and went into the kitchen. He tossed his coat and tie over a chair and followed her.

"What can I do to help?" he asked, looking around at her preparations with interest. Lettuce and tomatoes were on the counter, and broccoli was steaming in a pan on the stove. "Looks like I've put you to a lot of work," he said, gesturing ruefully.

"No, no, I enjoy it," Tilley insisted. "You could go outside and see how the fire's coming along, if you like." When he left the room, she put the thawed steaks on a platter and seasoned them with lemon pepper, garlic, and parsley.

"Looks good," David announced. "Shall I be the chief barbecuer?" He reached for the steaks.

"Sure thing," Tilley agreed happily, looking in a drawer for a long fork and an apron for him. "Go to it."

She could hear David humming to himself as he went back outside, and she felt the urge to join him, an odd happy little song catching in her throat. This seemed so natural, almost as if they did it every night. She bustled around, slicing up vegetables for a salad, mixing rice and cheese and broccoli into a hasty casserole and popping it into the oven. She had just pulled out a small stepstool to look for the wine when David appeared in the kitchen doorway. "Hey, what are you doing?" He leaned forward to place his hands on her waist to steady her as she stood on tiptoe to reach the bottle of Cabernet Sauvignon she'd been saving for so long.

"Your sommelier, at your service," she laughed. "My wine cellar's not as accessible as it might be, however."

She handed him the bottle and started to jump down, but David hastily put the wine down on the sink and reached for her waist, gently swinging her down in front of him, then drawing her close.

With a single, fluid movement, he gathered her in his arms, his lips on hers before she could say a word. She let herself go into that kiss, loving the sensation of surprise and arousal that David never failed to create in her. His mouth was warm and tender, and she parted her lips a bit, teasing him. They stood there for a long moment, lost in each other's arms, until finally Tilley drew back slightly. "Looks like you might burn dinner," she said breathlessly.

"Would it matter?" David asked before kissing her again. He nipped an earlobe playfully and said, "Be right back," without waiting for her answer.

Tilley set the table and began to carry out the food. When David returned with the steaks, dinner was almost ready. She got out two good wineglasses and handed David the bottle and corkscrew and moved the flowers he'd brought slightly away from the center of the table so they could see each other. He held out her chair for her with a flourish.

"Tell me, do you whip up wonderful dinners like this just any time?" David asked as he placed the napkin in his lap and passed her the salad.

"Only for special occasions and celebrations," Tilley replied, pouring the wine. "And when I don't get a delivery boy bringing chicken and basil from Renu's." She gave him a flirtatious smile.

"I'll make a note of that," David said. "This is so good I may be dropping in again."

"Any time," Tilley returned lightly.

Dinner was a complete success. They talked about the Easter egg hunt and the park, and about what would happen next. Afterward, Tilley made coffee and they moved to the sofa.

"Thanks, Tilley," David murmured appreciatively. "That was a lovely celebration."

She took a sip of her coffee before replying. "Don't thank me. It was your idea, after all." When he moved closer and stretched a long arm around her shoulders, she made no objection but settled comfortably back into the protective curve of his body. This is the way it should be, she thought with perfect pleasure.

The companionable silence had almost lulled her into a false sense of security, when David spoke. "You know, you and I have some serious talking to do, Tilley."

"Oh, no you don't," she said, raising a hand in objection. "I don't even want to think about candy—at least not until tomorrow. You don't know how hard holidays can be in this business."

"Candy wasn't exactly what I had in mind," David assured her. "We'll worry about that when the time is right."

Tilley looked at him askance. "Then what do we have to talk about?"

David leaned forward and gently kissed her cheek. "This." He ran a finger down the curve of her jaw. "And this." His warm breath caressed her ear. "And then there's always this."

Tilley had known this was coming, but she hadn't expected to feel the way she did about it. Each touch was like tender torture. She'd wanted David so badly for so long, and she'd tried so hard to talk herself out of it. But no reason could convince her, could make her stop wanting him. "Keep talking," she said softly. "You're doing fine." The darkness had begun to fill the room and the only light remaining was from the candles on the dinner table. Tilley felt almost as if she and David were cut off from the rest of the world, snug and cozy.

"Oh, Tilley," he said gruffly, his arms encircling her waist, then gently pushing her back into the soft cushions of the sofa. "I wish you knew how beautiful that smile of yours is, how your eyes light with fire when that red-headed temper of yours is set off. Don't you know what you do to a man?" He settled himself beside her, his lips meeting hers tenderly at first, then possessively, as if he alone had the right to that pleasure.

She caught his eager tongue and held it with a teasing ardor that matched his. When she arched her back slightly, she could feel her breasts against his strong chest, and her nipples stiffened immediately. David's lips moved to her ear for a nibble, then slowly made their way down the soft sensitive skin of her neck. His hand reached under her sweater to cup one lovely pear-shaped breast to his lips, his tongue teasing her rosy nipple. She drew her breath in sharply, knowing that they were crossing some barrier into the next stage of their relationship, and she only knew that she wanted this moment to go on forever.

"You don't know what you're doing to me," she murmured softly, a little embarrassed at her own response, her own need for him.

"Oh, I think I do," David assured her, kissing the corners of her mouth. "It's what you've been doing to me ever since I met you."

Tilley laughed, her heart gladdened by this open confession on his part, and she reached up to take his face between her hands and pull it down to hers. "I love what you do to me, David Danforth. I love—" The word came so easily to her lips that she stopped, a little frightened.

As if he knew what she was feeling, David kissed her again, and this time the kiss was a question, and she knew what the answer, the only answer, could be. This time there was no postponing the inevitable, no possibility for interruption, no hesitation about what should or might happen. They were simply a man and a woman who wanted each other desperately. They were in the right place at the right time, and there was the chance that they could have it all and it would be better than they had ever dreamed.

Tilley gently disengaged herself from the embrace, and got up and walked to the bedroom door. David hurried to catch up with her. "That's far enough," he said, sweeping her up in his arms. "You're not taking another step without me."

"I don't want to go anywhere without you," Tilley said boldly, her hands resting on his chest. She had no illusions. She knew exactly what she was doing, and she was a little surprised at her own eagerness. But there was nothing rational about her feelings, nothing that could be explained logically.

David took her in and gently placed her on the bed, undressing her slowly, leisurely, taking his time in caressing each part of her body. Tilley shivered a bit at his touch, her body alight with eager anticipation. David quickly joined her, undressing gracefully and confidently tossing his clothes over hers on the chair that stood by the bed. He looked deeply into her eyes for a moment, as if giving her a little more time to think about it, but Tilley simply held out her arms to him, no longer willing to wait another second.

Moments later, they were wrapped in each other's arms, tasting, savoring each other's desire. Tilley couldn't believe the tender storm David created over every inch of her skin. Every nerve in her body was screaming for closer contact, but David took his time. Finally, when she could wait no longer, she moved her legs restlessly, and David followed her unspoken bidding. He took charge, lowering his body to hers, and then it was as if there was no time or space outside the moment they were sharing. He seemed tireless in his efforts to please her, and Tilley held on for as long as she could, before swirling circles of ecstacy began to engulf her. "I love you," she whispered, not sure that he could hear her, but not caring. Surely he knew that now.

She watched with wonder as he took his pleasure. His eyes widened with delight as he moved within her, until finally he collapsed with a shudder into her soft comfort. They lay still for a moment, their bodies intertwined, their hearts beating as one. Tilley lay there beneath his warm body, comforted by his heavy weight, her arms wrapped around his neck, sleep only a moment away.

Suddenly, with no warning, David rolled over on his side, his eyes bright with an idea just taking hold. "That's it!" he said, as crisply as if he had just snapped his fingers. "Fireworks!"

"What are you talking about?" Tilley demanded, almost crossly.

"Firecrackers!" he answered as if that would explain all.

"Firecrackers! What on earth are you talking about?" Tilley turned over and rested on her elbows, looking down at David, who was now off in a world of his own. She had seen this look in his eye before, and she wasn't at all sure that she liked it.

"We can make candy firecrackers and sell them on the Fourth of July." He sat up in bed, buoyed by the excitement of his idea.

Tilley shook her head no. "No," she said adamantly. "That won't ever go. No one buys candy for the Fourth of July." She put her head down on the pillow.

"That used to be true," David said, equally sure of his position. "But not anymore. You're going to design a rock candy firecracker, and Danforth's will sell it. I can see it now—cinnamon and licorice. We'll display it all over the store—stars and stripes forever. It's better than apple pie!"

Tilley had to laugh at his boyish enthusiasm. It was one of his charms, one she found irresistible. In spite of her better judgment, she began to see the display through his eyes. "We can wrap each one in clear cellophane, twisted at the end like a stick of dynamite."

David turned to look at her, his eyes filled with devotion. "You see," he said huskily. "You do know how to make fireworks, Tilley. And so do I. Sparklers and Roman candles and shooting stars. . . ." He reached for her again.

6

What do you mean, he's in Southeast Asia?" Tilley demanded impatiently, cradling the phone between her shoulder and her left ear as she stirred a bowl of chocolate. "There must be some mistake. I just saw him last week. And I need to talk to him about this order for the Fourth of July." But even as she spoke, Tilley knew there was no mistake. David was gone. He hadn't even said goodbye.

The voice of David Danforth's secretary was cool and collected. "I'm sorry, Ms. Hart. All I can tell you is, he left here in a rush on a buying trip. It came up unexpectedly. He told me not to expect him back for another six weeks or so. For all I know, he could be in Hong Kong right now. But I'm sure he'll check in. I'll tell him you called."

Tilley paused for a moment, then spoke again in a

cooler voice. It wouldn't do to take her anger out on David's secretary. She was probably just a nice woman doing her job, and from what Tilley knew of David, it couldn't be an easy one. "No, that's all right. I'll manage. I'm sure he'll get in touch with me when he gets back. And thanks. I'm sorry I sounded so brusque."

"That's all right," the secretary sighed. "He has that effect on a lot of people."

I'll just bet he does, Tilley fumed to herself as she said goodbye and replaced the receiver. If he makes love to all his suppliers and then takes off for six weeks without a word, I bet she gets a lot of angry phone calls like this one. She stood there by the phone trying to decide what to do next. On the one hand, she simply couldn't believe that David had left without saying goodbye. On the other hand . . .

"Problems?" Jacques had come in and was preparing to get to work.

"Not really," Tilley sighed, pulling herself together. She had been such a fool! But she was determined not to let Jacques—or anyone, for that matter—know how hurt she was. This was one problem she'd have to work out for herself. "Not unless you call an order for two thousand candy firecrackers a problem." She hoped her voice sounded lighthearted.

"Ah, don't tell me," Jacques said. He tapped his forehead as if he were receiving messages from the beyond. "The merchandising genius has struck again, and this time for the Fourth of July."

"Right again," Tilley said, managing a laugh. "I'd hoped to have his advice on the design, but his secretary tells me he's in Southeast Asia somewhere and won't be back for six weeks."

Jacques eyed her thoughtfully. He was no longer clowning around. "That was sudden, wasn't it?"

Tilley looked at him sharply. How much did he know? "Yes, it was," she said simply, hoping to discourage any more questions. Later she could talk about it, when she'd sorted all this out for herself. Now she had to put on a good face. "Well, he'll just have to take whatever I come up with."

"And he should be glad to have it!" Jacques announced. "I've never known you to come up with a bad idea, Tilley."

Tilley gave him a grateful glance. She didn't know what she'd done to deserve having Jacques working for her, but whatever it was, she hoped she'd keep on doing it. "Thanks, Jacques," she said, forcing a smile. "Let's just hope this isn't the first time." She handed him the bowl of chocolate and left the kitchen, hoping she hadn't been too abrupt. It had been all she could do not to turn and run from the room.

Safely inside the studio, she shut the door behind her and leaned against it. I should have known, she said to herself angrily. The man's a Casanova. Anyone could have told me that. Anyone with any sense would never have gotten involved with him. How could she have been such a fool?

Well, never again, she told herself. Once. Not twice. In the meantime, she had an order to fill, a large one, unless, of course, he had changed his mind about that, too. She walked over to the drawing table and ran her fingers over the smooth surface. She picked up a pencil, twirling it between her fingers.

It didn't make any sense. Try as hard as she might, she just couldn't believe that David had used her. She sat down at the stool in front of the drawing table. He had felt something for her. She hadn't imagined it. She thought back to their picnic dinner at Danforth's, the Valentine's Day ball, the way he'd looked at her while they danced, the night he'd helped with the catalog . . . and then Easter, the night they'd become lovers. That had been real, it had to have been.

No, she said to herself sternly, you've got to stop this. You've got to face facts. It wasn't as important to him as it was to you. That's all there is to it. That's the chance you always take. She was beginning to get her second wind.

I won't let this be the end of my world, she said with firm resolve. It won't seem so bad with time, and I'll feel better in a couple of weeks. She took out a drawing pad and began fiddling with the ideas for the firecracker. The merchant prince wants firecrackers, I'll give him firecrackers. It'll be something to remember me by, something he won't ever forget.

Just then Amelia came in with a cup of coffee for her. "What's up, Tilley?" she asked brightly, tucking a strand of her long black hair behind one ear. "What are you working on? Jacques said you might want my help."

"You bet," Tilley said, just as brightly. "You're just the person I want to see." And she told her briefly about the order for Danforth's. "It's got to be simple but jazzy enough to catch a customer's eye."

"Okay," Amelia said, looking over Tilley's sketches.

"We can do that. Let's see, now. I like this one." And for the next couple of hours, the two worked on a design, drawing and sketching all sorts of different things—firecrackers exploding, Roman candles, strings of firecrackers, and elaborate designs for packaging.

"I can see why you're an art major," Tilley exclaimed approvingly, as she admired one of Amelia's sketches. "You've got a lot of talent."

"Thanks," Amelia said modestly, her broad smile betraying her pleasure. "But I feel like an amateur next to you. You've got some good ideas."

The two women spent the rest of the morning together, talking about the design for the firecracker, interrupted occasionally as one or the other went out to the front of the store to wait on customers. By the end of the day, they had come up with a design that they were both pleased with—a cinnamon firecracker with a licorice fuse, studded with nonpareils of red, white, and blue.

"It looks good," Tilley said proudly. "I just hope David Danforth hasn't bitten off more than he can chew. The Fourth of July isn't really a very good time to promote candy. People just don't associate the two things the way they do with other holidays."

"Well, if anyone can do it, David is the best bet. Anyway, you're just filling an order, Tilley. It's only business. He's the one who has to sell them."

"I know," she said glumly, getting her purse out of a drawer. "That's what I keep telling myself." But to herself she said, for all I know, David's forgotten all about this. In the grand scheme of things at Danforth's, this can't be a very important order. She sighed.

"Are you okay, Tilley?" Amelia looked concerned.

"What?" Tilley asked, so preoccupied that she had scarcely heard what was being said to her.

"I said, are you okay?" Amelia repeated, exchanging worried glances with Jacques.

"I'm fine, really I am," Tilley said hastily. "It's just been a long day. As soon as I take this order by the post office, I'm going to call it quits." She had just taken a telephone order and wanted to make sure it got out that night.

"Why don't you let me do that," Amelia said, taking the package from Tilley. "It's on my way, remember? You live here."

"And let me lock up," Jacques said, taking Tilley by the shoulders and turning her in the direction of the stairs. "You go upstairs and relax. Get your feet up and rest awhile. You're looking a little peaked."

Tilley did as she was told, glad to have some time to herself. She was feeling a little down and wasn't surprised that it showed. She only hoped no one guessed the real reason. The last thing she wanted at the moment was anyone's sympathy. She felt silly enough as it was without having to give any explanations.

The next six weeks flew by as Tilley threw herself into her work. She was determined to forget all about David Danforth. He wasn't worth it, she told herself. No man was. And though she knew that refrain had a hollow ring, she nevertheless repeated it to herself often. As usual, business at the Chocolate Moose was good, better than good, and Tilley had her hands full most of the time. She worked hard designing the new mold and doing some trial runs with Jacques for the firecracker candy. Amelia was working every day on the sketches for the new cookbook, and her spirits seemed to be rising steadily, much to everyone's relief. She still had a lot of catching up to do with her school work, but that was a mechanical problem. She could do it, they all knew, once she started getting over Billy Akers.

All in all, business was increasing, and Tilley was getting more organized to better cope with the demand. Despite all the new challenges, Tilley felt happier and more in control of her life than ever before.

All of her life, that is, except the part she had shared with David Danforth, whatever that was. She thought back to that night they'd spent together more than she cared to admit. How could she help it? Those damned firecrackers were a constant reminder. As the days went by without even a postcard, she knew she'd been a fool—just another name on that undoubtedly long list of his conquests. She wouldn't make the same mistake again, that was for sure. As it was, she just didn't have her heart in the firecracker project. But a deal was a deal, even if it wasn't made under the most businesslike circumstances.

"That's the last of them," Jacques grumbled one Saturday afternoon near the middle of June as he packed the final shipment of firecracker candy. The baskets, lined with red, white, and blue tissue paper, had been purchased especially for this candy, and Tilley would deliver them personally to David's office.

"And I for one am glad to be through," Tilley said, a note of real triumph in her voice. "All that's left is for me to deliver this to Danforth's. And then that's it!"

"This is one Independence Day I'm really going to appreciate," Rachel concluded wryly.

"You and me both," Tilley said with a grin.

When she locked up that night and went up to her apartment, it was with a feeling of intense relief. She had taken the candy to Danforth's—without a hitch. That was one chore she had been dreading, and now that it was behind her, she could really relax. The big push was over, at least for a while, and she was glad to have some breathing space. She spent the night celebrating, in her own quiet way, taking special care with the chicken curry she made for dinner.

She made a beautiful fruit salad with her favorite honey dressing, even breaking out a bottle of Chablis for herself, a rare treat. Tilley had learned from long experience that living alone was made up of these small pleasures, and she knew that she deserved something special after all the weeks of hard work.

She spent the rest of the evening determinedly ignoring anything to do with work, sipping mint tea, and reading a torrid best seller, and when midnight came around, she was ready for bed, enjoying the promise of sleeping late the next morning and a whole day ahead with nothing but fun scheduled. The Park People were having a ground-breaking ceremony for the playground at Parker Park the next day, and she was really looking forward to it, even though it reminded her of David.

Just as she was snuggling up with a pillow, there was a soft thump at the window. Tilley opened her eyes. There it was again. Thump. What on earth? Tilley rolled over on her back. Surely she was just imagining the noise. Or maybe it was a car out in the street. She lay there for a minute, still listening. She could hear the traffic over on Kirby.

She turned back over and closed her eyes. This time the noise was a thud. Tilley sat up in bed and looked at the French doors that opened out on the terrace. For the first time, she felt a shiver of fear. There it was again. Tilley's eyes widened. That sounded like a rock, she thought. Throwing the covers aside, she crawled out of bed, and throwing on her bathrobe, she tiptoed to the door. She was about to pull back the sheer curtains and look out when there was another crash. This time she was certain it was a rock.

By now she was getting angry. Any minute she could be surrounded by breaking glass. She was opening the door when she heard a soft call. "Tilley, are you there?"

She knew who it was even before her foot touched the terrace. Her heart stopped beating. David. It was David. She raced to the low wall that surrounded the sun porch and looked over. "David Danforth, is that you?"

"At your service, madam." He took a couple of steps back and looked up at her. He had on blue jeans, white tennis shoes, and a polo shirt.

"You've got a lot of nerve," Tilley flung down at him, her voice just barely above a whisper. She pulled her silk bathrobe close over her nightgown.

"Not really." He shook his head. "I was afraid if I called, you'd hang up. And if I came during the day, there would be a thousand people around. I need to talk to you, Tilley. This seemed like the only way." He was talking normally now, his voice carrying through the night air.

"Shhhhh," Tilley whispered. "Someone will hear you."

"There's no one around to hear us," David said, holding out his hands. "I made sure Pepper's truck was gone."

"Well, it doesn't matter. I don't have anything to say to you." She was still whispering. "Unless of course, you have a question about the candy. And in that case, you can call me at the office. If you've forgotten the number, it's in the book." Her voice was cold. She had no intention of falling prey to his shenanigans. Her heart had started beating again, and she was completely in charge of her emotions.

"You know I don't want to talk about candy," he called out. "I want to talk about you and me." There was a plea in his voice.

"You've got to be crazy," she whispered furiously. She knew she should go back into her room and close the door. She shouldn't stand there and talk to him. It could only lead to more trouble. "What's there to talk about? You left without so much as calling to say goodbye, it's been nice knowing you. And that says all I want to hear. You don't have to add insult to injury." Good sense wasn't having much luck getting her off the terrace. Something in her wanted to hear what he had to say.

"I've got a lot of explaining to do, I know. If you'll just let me in, I'll—"

"Let you in?" Tilley leaned on the railing. "I did that once, remember? And all it got me was a lot of heartache. Just go knock on someone else's door. You probably have a lot of names in a little black book somewhere. Just leave me out of it." There was real vehemence in her voice, and she turned as if to leave.

"No, Tilley, please don't go. I'll stay out here all night if I have to," he pleaded. He was standing out in the middle of the street. "Would it help if I got down on my knees?"

"Don't be silly," Tilley began. A pair of headlights turned on the street. David was spotlighted in a pool of light, and a police car stopped not two feet from where he was standing.

Instinctively David held up his hands. A policeman got out of the car and walked over to David. "What's going on?" he asked, and his voice was sharp.

David lowered his hands a little sheepishly. "It's nothing, officer," he started to explain. "I left my keys at home. Locked myself out. I was just waking up the little lady. She's about to let me in."

The policeman looked at him doubtfully.

"Really," David said earnestly, looking up at Tilley. "Isn't that right, Tilley?"

A second policeman turned off the car lights and got out of the car. They both looked up at Tilley. "Is this man bothering you?" the first one called out. He directed a flashlight to the terrace.

Tilley squinted against the bright light. She was silent for a minute, as if she had a choice. Then, with a sardonic look at David, who was looking up at her innocently, she said, "It's okay, officer. I was just about to come down and let him in."

"See?" David said, holding up his hands. "What did I tell you?"

The policeman looked at him skeptically. "You just make sure this doesn't happen again. You gotta be careful, you know. These streets aren't safe at night."

"Yes, sir," David agreed seriously. "And thank goodness you fellows were on the ball. We all sleep better . . ." Tilley couldn't hear anything else as she turned and hurried down the stairs. She'd been had and she knew it. She unlocked the front door and took off the chain. When she opened the door, David was still talking to the policemen.

"Isn't that right, darling?" he said, when he saw her at the door. He shook the policeman's hand and turned to come in.

"Oh, I'm sure of it," she said sweetly, holding the door open for him. To the policeman she said, "He has a very strong sense of civic duty, gentlemen. If you're not careful, he'll talk all night." She folded her arms and impatiently tapped one foot.

"She's always like that when she wakes up," David explained with a wave as he entered the store. He leaned down and kissed Tilley.

She was leaning against the closed door as the police drove away. David stood in front of her, his hands in his pockets. Neither spoke for a moment. They just looked at each other silently.

"Are you sure you didn't plan this?" Tilley asked

suspiciously, a hint of a smile flickering around her mouth. She looked at him solemnly.

David grinned. "For a moment there, I thought you were going to—"

"I should have," Tilley interrupted. "I should have let you talk yourself out of that one. That's what you deserve."

"God, it's good to see you," David said, completely ignoring what she said and taking one step closer.

Tilley looked up at him. If he'd never come this close, she might have been able to stand her ground. But all she had to do was reach out and touch him. He was there, and her heart cried out. Nothing else mattered. "I must be the one who's crazy," she said hopelessly, as he gathered her up in his arms.

"Oh, Tilley," he murmured, "it's been such a long time. Can you ever forgive me?" But his lips wouldn't wait for an answer.

Tilley made no resistance, not even a token one, but allowed herself to savor the kiss, to give in to the feelings of loneliness she had experienced ever since he'd left. The pressure of his lips and his tongue's urgent exploration of her mouth all but told her that she'd been wrong, that there had been some mistake. This was the same David who held her in his arms, made love to her. This was the man she laughed with, danced with, worked with. This was the man she thought she'd lost.

"So what happened?" she asked when he finally released her, her head next to his, her body warm against his. It was real. It wasn't a dream.

"I don't know," he said, wearily, then with more

conviction, he added, "No, that's not true. I do know what happened. I was scared, absolutely terrified. I'm falling in love with you, Tilley, and it scares me to death."

Tilley stood where she was, her arms still folded, her eyes on David, her face expressionless. "I don't know how you expect me to believe that," she said, but she knew he was telling the truth. "One postcard, one phone call would have been enough."

"I know, I know," David said, running a hand through his hair. "I called once," he admitted, not too happily, "but you weren't in. Rachel answered, at least I think it was Rachel. I was afraid she'd recognized my voice. I didn't even leave my name."

Tilley's heart leapt with joy. "But that doesn't make any sense, David—"

David silenced her lips with his fingers. "I know it doesn't. I don't know how I expect you to understand it." He kissed her forehead gently. "Everywhere I went, I saw your face, heard your voice, your laughter. I can't run away from it, Tilley. The world's just not big enough."

Tilley closed her eyes and held him close. She was quiet for what seemed like a long time. "Are you okay, Tilley?" David finally asked. He pulled back and, holding her at arm's length, tilted her face up to his, his hand on her chin.

When she opened her eyes, they were filled with tears. But she was smiling, her heart racing, keeping time to a new song. "I should probably have my head examined," she said quietly, shaking her head, "but—" She hesitated. "But I'd be lying if I said I wasn't glad to see you." She moved her fingers over his face, gently tracing the features so familiar, so long absent from her life. "Welcome back," she whispered.

"Oh, I have so many things to tell you," David said, his face filled with relief. "I was afraid you'd never speak to me again. I was afraid—"

Tilley cut him short. "Don't, David," she said, pulling him close. She held him for a moment. Then she said simply, "Let's go upstairs." She looked up at him. "I've got a lot to tell you, too." Then she grinned.

David tucked her arm around his waist, put his arm around her shoulder. "It's good to be back, Tilley," he said as they headed for the stairs.

She nodded. "We've got a lot of catching up to do."

He grinned, that old mischievous expression a welcome sight. "Wait'll you hear what I've dreamed up for Christmas. If you think those firecrackers were a great idea—"

"Oh, David," Tilley stopped in protest. Then she laughed. "I guess we have to start somewhere," she teased as they continued upstairs. "We might as well start with business."

7

Tilley tossed her white straw shoulder bag onto the seat next to her as she got into the car. The interior of the small orange VW was very hot, and Tilley rolled down the window, giving the car's air conditioning a minute to get working. It was July, a typically hot, muggy day. All of Houston was sweltering in the oppressive heat, and Tilley was glad she had chosen her coolest summer outfit this morning. It was nearly three o'clock in the afternoon, and she still felt fresh and cool in the navy seersucker dress with its long white sailor collar and her red high-heeled sandals.

When the air conditioner began to work its magic, she rolled up the window and backed out of the parking lot next to the Chocolate Moose. Southhampton's Hardware Store across the street was doing a brisk business, and Tilley noted with some satisfaction that there were no parking places left in front of the Chocolate Moose.

She stopped at the stop sign at the end of the street. Watching as the cars whizzed by on Kirby, she reached into her purse for her sunglasses. The glare of the sun on the pavement was intense, and her eyes relaxed behind the protective dark tint. It was the day after the Fourth of July, and she was on her way to Danforth's to shop at the traditional holiday sale.

Humming softly to herself, she thought back through the past couple of weeks. Business was better than ever, and Tilley had her hands full keeping up with it. "And to think I wanted a quiet little store," she had said to Jacques only the week before when she'd hired two new part-time salespeople to help out up front. Fortunately, it was easy to find help with so many teenagers out of school. She hadn't decided what she'd do in the fall after school started. Not only would she lose the school kids, but Amelia and Rachel would be seniors.

Tilley pushed her sunglasses back up on her nose. That was one bridge she'd have to cross when she got to it. There was an opening in the traffic, and she turned onto Kirby, skillfully making her way down the busy street. Amelia had taken to the cookbook illustrations like a duck to water. It had been just the thing to take her mind off her troubles. Billy Akers was all but forgotten. Amelia had soon begun staying late, working in the studio after hours on the preliminary sketches, and it hadn't been long before Amelia and Pepper were bending over the drawing boards together until all hours of the morning.

David was also intrigued by the idea of the cookbook,

though he couldn't help being chagrined that he hadn't thought of it himself. "It's a natural," he had said excitedly. "And Danforth's will sell it." They had gone to Galveston for supper and were celebrating Independence Day with boiled shrimp and ice cold beer at the Balinese Room overlooking the warm Gulf waters. Tiny sailboats dotted the horizon, and a tugboat was pulling an ocean liner out to sea.

"You don't suppose there's any chance it could be ready by November, do you—in time for the opening of the London store?" he asked eagerly.

Tilley had laughed at his transparency. She knew by now that he judged the rest of the world by what it could do for Danforth's. It was not an unpleasant trait for all its persistence. "No, David, it's going to take longer than that."

"That's what I was afraid of," he said regretfully, "but it was a nice thought."

Tilley reached across the table and covered his hand with hers. "It is a nice thought, but it'll still be a nice thought next Christmas."

David lifted his glass of beer in a toast. "Christmas after next—and I can relax, secure in the knowledge that no other store has candy to equal ours. By that time, the Chocolate Moose candy will be a Danforth's exclusive."

"Aren't you taking a lot for granted?" Tilley asked, looking at him over the rim of her glass.

"We have a deal, remember? You said you'd think seriously about signing a contract with me after the Fourth of July." David folded his arms on the table and leaned forward to kiss her. "I'm having the papers drawn up to give you in the next couple of days."

Tilley met him halfway across the table, her lips touching his in a kiss. "Oh, no, that's not what I said. I said we'd see how the firecrackers fare, our trial run."

"Details, details," David said with a grin. "Don't bother me with details."

"Which reminds me—how are the firecrackers doing?" She took a sip of her beer. David hadn't mentioned the promotion in some time, and she was curious—not that she was in any way involved. Danforth's had made a special order, and she had fulfilled the store's specifications. Her part of the deal was over.

But David had been noncommittal, saying only that it was too soon to tell. He hadn't yet gotten a full report from his floor manager, but he would in the next day or so. "For now," he'd said teasingly, "I have a different sort of fireworks in mind—yours and mine. Let's go home."

Tilley smiled to herself as she turned onto Shepherd, a slight blush on her face at the memory. She and David had been almost inseparable since his return from the buying trip, and Tilley didn't regret a moment of it. She had never known a man like David Danforth. His energy, his intelligence, his enthusiasm, and his good humor all worked together to make her feel like someone special when she was with him. She enjoyed their long talks after dinner, and their lovemaking never ceased to amaze her. They seemed so right together, so comfortable, even beyond the extraordinary physical attraction they had for each other. It seemed perfect, all of it, and for a moment, Tilley had a strange sense of foreboding. Maybe it was too good to be true.

Nonsense! Tilley admonished herself as she turned into the Danforth's parking lot. Don't start getting super-stitious. After all, some things *are* made in heaven. She pulled into a parking space and turned off the engine. Looking in the rearview mirror, she checked her lipstick and hair. Her red curls were held in place with a pair of ivory combs, and her makeup was fine. What's more, she felt as good as she looked.

As she walked through the heavy glass door, she realized that she was actually looking forward to buying some new clothes. It had been ages since she'd been shopping, and it was high time she treated herself to something new. As she met the cool air of the store and her eyes grew accustomed to the interior lighting, her first thought was to see if there were any remnants of the firecracker display, though she realized the holiday deco-rations had probably been taken down the night before when the sale signs had gone up.

But Danforth's was a lovely store, and she was easily distracted by the racks of dresses, many of them reduced to half their original price. Unable to resist such bargains, Tilley quickly thumbed through the racks, looking for her size, and when she first saw the basketful of candy firecrackers, she was carrying an armful of dresses.

"I don't believe it!" she said out loud to no one in particular. She had rounded a corner and was within inches of a display of the candy firecrackers. But it wasn't what she'd expected. All along the candy counter were straw baskets filled with the candy firecrackers—all marked down to a penny apiece!

Tilley stopped dead in her tracks, her heart seized with pain. She might as well have seen her own children sold off into slavery. That's how bad she felt. She'd been right in the first place. The Fourth of July was no time to sell candy. Why, oh why had she let herself be caught up in one of David Danforth's promotions? She should have heeded her own instincts. This was the very thing she'd feared. They'd gone too far too fast. The fireworks had fizzled.

There was only one thing to do, that much was obvious. Handing the dresses to a saleswoman who happened to be passing by, she strode off to find whoever was selling the candy.

"Pardon me, don't you want to try these on?" the astonished saleswoman called after her. Tilley had all but thrown the clothes at her, and the other woman was staggering from the unexpected weight.

"I don't have time now. I'm sorry." Tilley didn't even stop. She had other things on her mind now, more pressing business. The shopping spree was all but forgotten.

"May I help you?" The young woman behind the candy counter was pleasant enough. Her long blond hair was pulled back with a ribbon, and she wore thick eyeglasses that gave her an intellectual air.

"I certainly hope so," Tilley answered immediately, setting her purse down on the counter in front of her. "I want to buy every piece of that candy," she explained, pointing to the baskets. "Right now. I'll pay you double the price if you'll have it taken off the floor within the hour." Tilley didn't mince words. She knew her own mind.

"Now? Right this minute?" The young woman was still not convinced. "All of it?"

"That's right," Tilley acknowledged as patiently as she knew how. She was in no mood to explain her actions. She was the customer and the customer was always right—but she didn't want to take her anger and disappointment out on this young woman. She was only doing her job. "They *are* for sale, I assume?"

"Oh, yes, ma'am. They're for sale—they have been for some time now, but it hasn't been what you'd call a hot item." She was still staring at Tilley, making no move to sell her the candy. She ventured a laugh, having no way of knowing that was the last thing Tilley wanted to hear.

"Well, then," Tilley prompted, her temper threatening to flare, "what do I have to do to buy them?"

The young woman seemed slightly perplexed, but now she realized that Tilley meant what she said. This was not a practical joke. She looked over at the candy, thinking over the complications of such a sale. "I'm afraid we've got to count it," she said slowly, "and that's going to take some time."

"Too much," Tilley said without hesitation. She didn't relish the idea of someone standing there laboriously counting the candy piece by piece. What she wanted was to get the whole lot out of sight as soon as possible, regardless of the cost.

"From the looks of it, I'd say Danforth's hasn't sold a

tenth of its stock." She put her hands on her hips and studied the baskets of candy, all the while making some mental calculations. "I'll tell you what," she said finally, turning to the woman behind the counter. And she made what she knew was a fair offer—more than fair, in fact. She knew how many pieces she'd sold to the department store.

The young woman seemed relieved that she wouldn't have to count the candy. "But I'll have to check with my supervisor," she explained graciously. By this time, she had recovered from her initial surprise and was very businesslike.

"You do that," Tilley said crisply. "And take this." She handed the charge card to the young woman and directed her to have the candy delivered to the Chocolate Moose. "I have some other business to attend to in the store. I'll stop by on my way out. You do understand that I want this candy removed from the floor at once—the instant your supervisor approves the sale?"

"Oh, yes, ma'am," the young woman replied sincerely. "I understand completely. You can count on it." She looked down at the card in her hand. "Tilley Hart?" she said, then the name apparently registered. She looked back up at Tilley. "You're the candy maker, aren't you? The one who made all those Easter eggs."

"That's right," Tilley said, nodding her head affirmatively. She should have known she couldn't pull this off and remain anonymous at the same time. But she didn't want to get into a longer conversation, so her next words were to the point. "Now if you don't need me anymore, I'll go finish up my business here."

She turned and headed for David's office, hoping she hadn't been too rude. As she made her way through the crowded store, she knew she had overreacted. And she knew she should be more hard-nosed about the failure. It had to happen sooner or later. Business was business, after all. But her candy was more to her than business. It was a product she believed in, and she was proud of it. If she hadn't been a little sentimental in the first place, she might never have left New York and started her own business. And if she hadn't let her better judgment get lost in David's enthusiasm, this would never have happened. She knew what was best for the Chocolate Moose, and she should never have gotten sidetracked.

When she entered the suite of plush offices, the receptionist—a plump round woman in a beige shirtwaist dress—was answering the phone. Tilley paced the floor restlessly, her sandaled feet sinking into the thick soft carpet as she tried not to seem too impatient. The woman obviously had an irate customer on the phone, and Tilley didn't want to seem to be breathing down her neck. Just at that moment, a door opened, and a tall elegant woman walked out into the waiting room. She was wearing a long slinky beaded dress with a white fox stole around her shoulders. Behind her was another woman, similarly attired in evening dress. Her voluptuous figure was wrapped in pale blue satin and her black hair swept up in braids around her beautiful face.

Tilley stepped back, feeling a little childlike in her sailor collar. Next to these two glamorous women, she felt simple and unsophisticated. Silently she vowed never to wear this dress again, and for a moment her thoughts returned to the clothes she had handed to the hapless clerk. This certainly hasn't been my day, she thought ruefully.

Both women were laughing gaily as they walked out of the office, and right behind them was David Danforth himself.

"I'm sooo glad you like them," the second woman cooed. "But we've got two more really wonderful dresses to show you, don't we, Sue Ann?" She turned to her companion.

"Absolutely," Sue Ann concurred, her long black lashes flickering seductively. "And don't you worry," she said to David, "we'll be back up in a jiffy. It will only take a minute to change."

"I'll be expecting you then," David replied, his deep voice soft and melodious. "And thanks a lot. You've answered all my questions."

Tilley stood up to her full height, and clearing her throat, she caught David's attention. "Hello, Tilley!" he exclaimed, clearly glad to see her, but somewhat surprised. "What are you doing here?"

Tilley waited while the models left the waiting room, sure that the expression on her face was worth a thousand words. Finally, turning to David, she replied with some irony, "I hope I'm not interrupting something?"

"Heavens, no," David said, "and even if you were, I'd welcome it. You can interrupt me anytime." He put his hand on her waist and guided her into his office, shutting the door behind them.

"Now, what can I do for you?" he asked, kissing her

lightly on the lips. "It's too late for lunch and besides"—
he looked down at her, seeming to sense her tenseness—
"you look like you just lost your best friend." He held her
chin gently with his hand, a questioning look on his face.
"It can't be that bad."

Tilley decided to skip the amenities. "Why didn't you
tell me you were practically giving away my firecrackers?
Is this the kind of detail you don't want to be bothered
with?"

He blanched. He clearly hadn't expected this, but he
was prepared to explain. "I just learned about it this
morning. I haven't had a chance to tell you."

"I bet!" Tilley said, folding her arms impatiently across
her breasts and turning away from him. "Now I understand why you were so noncommittal last night. You
hadn't had a full report from your floor manager." She
mimicked his tone of voice. "And I fell for it. I really did."

"Tilley Hart, what's come over you?" he asked,
walking over to her and putting his arms around her. "So
we didn't sell as many firecrackers as I'd hoped we
would. It's not the end of the world."

Tilley was in no mood to be humored. "It may not be
the end of the world for you. *I'm* the one with egg all over
my face. It's my design, remember? My candy!" She
worked her way free of his embrace.

"Tilley, this isn't like you! You've got enough business
sense to know that everything can't be a roaring success." He shrugged his shoulders. "You win some, you
lose some."

"And some get rained out," she said with a scowl.
Then, knowing how unreasonable she was being, she

relented. "Look, David, that's a suitable policy for a store like Danforth's. This piece of merchandise is only a small part of your inventory. No one will notice Danforth's mistake, and if they do, it's a trivial matter." Her voice was much calmer now.

"I don't run a big business. I run a very small, very select candy store. My product is excellent, and that's what my customers expect. My inventory is small, and each item counts for a lot. I can't afford to make mistakes like this one. And to make matters worse, you've got my failure plastered all over the store." She shook her head. "Selling my candy for a penny! That's an insult!"

David had heard enough. "I bought that candy from you, if I remember correctly, and paid a good bit for it." Anger was creeping into his voice. "It's my money that was lost—not yours."

Tilley took one step closer and said softly, "And if I'd known this is the way you do business, I'd never have sold it to you."

David was clearly exasperated but seemed to be trying to make amends. "Okay, so maybe we should have had a better understanding. That's what these contracts are for," he said, indicating a stack of papers on his desk. "We can work out all the details in advance. You can tell me never to mark down the price on Chocolate Moose candy—next time. What's done is done."

"No, there'll be no contract, David. I'll be more than happy to sell you any quantity of candy that we already have in stock, like the chocolate moose you've bought for Christmas, but no more special orders. And I'm going to continue being my own distributor. I don't think you can do a better job of selling candy than I can. I wish you could see that." She walked over to the large plate glass window that looked down at the street.

David came up behind her, his hands resting on her shoulders. "Tilley, don't make any decisions right this minute. You're not yourself. You'll feel differently about all this tomorrow." He leaned down and kissed the back of her neck. "I don't know what I can do about all this now, unless of course you want me to get the candy off the floor."

Tilley turned and walked across the room, still refusing his gestures of affection. "That won't be necessary," she replied evenly. "I've already taken care of that."

"You what?" David was astonished.

"I bought it all back," Tilley explained, "and I had it delivered to the Chocolate Moose."

David shook his head in disbelief. "You didn't," he said quietly, as the truth of the situation hit him. And then he laughed.

There was something about his laughter that was contagious. "I did," she said, "I really did." Suddenly she could see herself swooping down on the candy counter, gathering up all her candy. There was something comical about it. A slow smile was beginning to break across her face.

David looked at Tilley tenderly. "That's what I like about you, Tilley Hart, you take the bull by the horns every time." He walked over to her, taking her in his arms. This time he wouldn't be pushed away. "I don't know what I ever did without you." And then he kissed her, hard, possessively, passionately—before he apologized. "I'm sorry, Tilley. I can see that it's important to you. Maybe I've been in this business too long. Failures hurt, some more than others."

Tilley eyed him suspiciously. "Do you mean that?"

"Of course I do," David answered earnestly. "It took me a while to realize how important this is to you. I didn't mean to be insensitive."

His apology was sincere, and Tilley knew it. She didn't pull away. "Thank you, David," she said softly, her fingers toying with his tie. "It means a lot to me that you understand. Someday I'll laugh about this, but not today." His words had had a soothing effect on her, and she was already beginning to feel better.

"I know," David said, his voice resonant with understanding. "And you don't have to laugh about it today—I promise." He leaned over and kissed her on the lips, his touch gentle but intense. When he pulled away, he looked down at her thoughtfully. "What do you say we get away from it all—just you and me. We'll walk right out of here as if neither one of us had a care in the world."

In spite of her wounded spirits, Tilley laughed, relieved that he wasn't trying to reason with her. "That sounds wonderful, Mr. Danforth, but if I remember correctly, you have a date with two very beautiful women." She raised her eyebrows flirtatiously.

David hit his forehead with his hand. "Oh, damn! The cover for the Christmas catalog. I forgot all about it."

Tilley wound her arms around his neck, kissing him on

the nose. "I'll tell you what," she said, "if I had another hour downstairs, I'd probably feel a lot better. A new dress does wonderful things for me."

"An hour it is," David said gratefully. "That ought to give me time to finish up here." He looked at his watch. "How about meeting me at the front door at four forty? We'll paint the town red."

Tilley was walking with him to the door. "We don't have to overdo this, David. Dinner and a show will do nicely." She stopped at the door and turned to him. "And David, thanks for being so understanding."

David opened the door for her. "Don't mention it—now," he said. "Save it for later. Dessert maybe?"

The two models were waiting outside, joking with the receptionist. Tilley looked from the models to David. Then she smiled and said sweetly, "Why don't we make that forty-five minutes?"

David smiled, his brown eyes meeting hers directly. "You've got yourself a deal," he answered. And Tilley thought they understood each other perfectly.

8

Oh, these are lovely, Amelia," Tilley exclaimed with genuine pleasure. "They're perfect!" She was looking through Amelia's preliminary sketches for the cookbook. It was Monday morning, and Tilley had been in the store since daybreak working on a large order that had to be delivered that afternoon. She had a lot on her mind but was glad to take a few minutes to work with Amelia.

"I like this one especially," Amelia ventured almost shyly, tossing her shiny black hair back over one shoulder. She turned the pages until she found her favorite. "I thought this might be good for the cover."

"Or this one back here." Tilley flipped back through the pages. "I love these colors." The two had spent the last thirty minutes poring over the illustrations, and Tilley was excited all over again about the book, pleased that

Amelia was having such a good time. The whole staff was relieved to see Amelia actually enjoying life again. "You're very good, Amelia. In fact, I'd say you're the best! Now, if I can just finish up with the recipes, we'd be in business." Tilley looked lovely in trim khaki pants and a pale green silk shirt.

Amelia reached for her cup of coffee. "You know, you might get Rachel to put those on the computer. It'd be a lot easier to make changes that way—and to keep track of them all." She wore a crisp yellow sundress with a wide white belt around her waist.

Tilley nodded. "I know. I've been thinking of buying a computer for the store. I think we could really use it around here, for bookkeeping, of course, but it would be great for the very thing you're talking about." She leaned on the counter thoughtfully.

"Not to mention what it'd do for Rachel," Amelia said with a grin. "What would she do with all that computer time?"

"We wouldn't have to wonder where she is," Tilley admitted with a laugh. "I'm sure I'd get to see a lot of her."

"That's an understatement, if I ever heard one." Amelia took a sip of her coffee. "Seriously, though, she'd know how to set it all up for you. What she doesn't know about computers isn't worth knowing."

"I've thought about that," Tilley responded honestly. "You two are my most important natural resources. I don't know what I'm going to do when you graduate." She shook her head with real desolation.

"Oh, you'll think of something," Amelia said sympathetically. "Besides, who says you're going to get rid of us so easily? Who knows? Maybe we'll decide to go to graduate school. It's not going to be easy, giving up this candy store." It was obvious that she meant what she was saying.

"Thanks, Amelia," Tilley said earnestly. "I'm glad to hear you say that. I'd hate to think this was just another job for you two. I can't imagine this place without you. Not that I think you can stay here forever. You've both got your own place to make in the world, and that's important to me, too."

Just at that moment, the front door opened, the bells ringing noisily. Both Amelia and Tilley looked up from their work. They had both been so engrossed in their conversation that they hadn't seen David walk up and were pleasantly surprised when he entered the store. He was wearing a white summer suit, a sand-colored dress shirt and matching tie, and a white straw fedora, its classical styling a perfect match for his elegance. He was carrying a leather briefcase in one hand.

"Good morning," Tilley sang out, glad to see him.

Amelia let out a long low whistle. "Now that's a class act if I ever saw one," she said to Tilley. "He's okay." She nodded approvingly.

Tilley grinned, not about to be outdone. "He's better than okay," was her quick reply. She smiled at David. It had been a week since the afternoon Tilley had raised such a fuss over the candy firecrackers, and though they'd talked often on the phone, she hadn't seen him since that night. Both had been swamped with work, and he was getting ready to spend the next six weeks in London. "What brings you to this neck of the woods?" she asked lightly.

"*You* bring me to this neck of the woods, as if you didn't know it." David took off his hat and winked at Amelia before walking over to Tilley. He put his briefcase down on the floor beside the counter and leaned over to give her a kiss.

"Don't tell me you're canceling our dinner date?" she asked, opening her eyes.

"Not on your life. I want to get some business out of the way so that we can have the evening all to ourselves. We've got to make some big plans—like when you're coming over and how many weeks you're going to stay."

"Weeks?" Tilley laughed good-naturedly. "Now that's what I call optimism. If I'm able to get away for a weekend, I'll be lucky."

"Don't listen to a word she says, David," Amelia interjected. "She's got a great staff around here. Why, we could run this store blindfolded if she'd let us."

"Oh, no you don't," Tilley retorted. "You've got all you can do keeping up with your summer school classes. I don't want you to be behind in English when school starts in the fall."

Amelia sighed, her forehead creased in thought. "You and Pepper are one of a kind. At the rate I'm going, I'll be able to win a Pulitzer prize. He wouldn't be satisfied if I wrote an essay a night."

"Well, that's what I like to hear," Tilley said firmly.

"And I'm going to see to it that you keep up with that schedule. You listen to Pepper. He knows what he's talking about."

David was looking through the sketches. "What have we here?" He was obviously impressed.

"Aren't they wonderful?" Tilley said, seeing the look of appreciation on his face. "Amelia has really outdone herself."

David turned the sketches so he could look through them. For a few minutes, he turned the pages silently, his full attention on the drawings. When he looked up, he turned to Amelia. "These are really very good."

She chuckled. "You sound a little surprised."

"Well, I guess I am," David said candidly. "I'm used to paying professionals a lot to do this for me."

Tilley turned to Amelia, a look of mock horror on her face. "David thinks no one can do anything as well as Danforth's." To David she said, "And I'll have you know Amelia's getting paid well for this, which makes her every bit the professional."

David had the good grace to be embarrassed. "Well, I, ah . . ."

Tilley and Amelia both laughed of one accord. "We know," Tilley said, playfully twisting his nose. "You're sorry. You didn't mean to be patronizing."

David rolled his eyes up to the ceiling. "Now that I've got my foot in my mouth, it's hard to start over."

Tilley came from behind the counter. "That's okay," she said affectionately. "Just don't let it happen again." She kissed him. "Now—what can I do for you?"

David bent over and picked up his briefcase. "Well, now that you mention it, I do have something—"

"Tilley, I've got to have a word with you." Jacques interrupted their conversation in an unusual display of temper. "Now." His cheeks were red, and he made no attempt to hide his annoyance.

Tilley turned to him, surprised. "Sure, Jacques. What is it?"

"This recipe doesn't work. I've tried it three times this morning, and each time the syrup refuses to harden. I've never seen anything like it."

"Let me see that," Tilley asked, reaching for the notecard. It was unlike Jacques to be so frustrated. She couldn't imagine what the matter was. "Oh, the Bordeaux chocolate." She studied the recipe for a minute. "It looks all right to me," she said, a little puzzled. "What kind of sugar are you using?"

"Granulated, superfine. What else would I use?" He shrugged his shoulders in exasperation. He was clearly stumped and didn't like it one bit.

Tilley could see that it was time for tact. "Look, if you'll give me just a minute, I'll come in and try it with you. Maybe the measurements were copied down wrong. Go do something else. Surely this isn't the only thing on your agenda."

Jacques snorted. "No, of course not. I just don't like to admit defeat, that's all."

David had been leaning against the counter all this time. "I can't even imagine it, Jacques. There must be something wrong with the recipe."

Jacques turned to David, realizing that he was in the room for the first time. "Oh, good morning, David. It's good to see you." He threw his hands up in the air. "And don't mind me. I'm just an old man who was up too late last night. Pepper came over and read his latest poems. They were good and we forgot about the time. Guess I'm paying for it now."

"They are good, aren't they?" Amelia chimed in. Then she looked bashfully at everyone. "He read them to me too," she added unnecessarily.

"Uh oh," Tilley said softly, her eyes on the front door. "Back to work, you guys. We've got more customers."

Jacques took the cue. "Guess I'll make some more of that toffee we ran out of yesterday. I can do that with one hand tied behind my back." He turned and headed back to the kitchen, whistling as he walked.

The bells on the door were ringing again when Tilley turned to David. "I'm sorry. The whole morning has been like this." She looked over at Amelia. "I really like the illustrations. Let's talk about them some more later."

"You bet," Amelia agreed, hurrying off to take care of the new customers.

"Now, where were we?" Tilley said to David, taking him by his arm.

He leaned over and kissed her. Then he picked up his briefcase again. "This will only take a minute, I promise," he said easily.

"Let's go in the studio. That might give us a few minutes alone." She pulled him after her into the relative quiet of the back room.

"I just wanted to leave these contracts with you," David said, shutting the door behind him. "I knew you'd want a chance to look over them."

"What contracts?" Tilley asked, her voice a shade crisper.

"The contracts I had drawn up, of course. I had them ready for you the other day, but you weren't in any mood to see them, if I remember correctly." He pulled out a large sheaf of paper.

Tilley froze. There had to be some mistake. "I remember correctly if you don't." Then a new thought occurred to her, and she relaxed immediately. "Oh, I know. You're talking about the purchase orders for the chocolate moose. I thought for a second you were talking about being my distributor again." She walked over to him and took the papers from him. "For a minute there, you had me worried." She smiled up at him, but her attention had already turned to the papers in her hand.

"Well, I'm talking about both, of course," David replied casually. "That top one is the purchase order for the Christmas candy—one for Houston, one for London. The contract is underneath." He was now looking over her shoulder.

Tilley looked up at him. "David," she began quietly, "I'll be more than glad to accept the purchase orders. We've already started on that, and you'll have the chocolate moose in plenty of time for the opening of the new store." Then she hesitated, not sure where to begin. "But I said last week I wasn't interested in a contract with Danforth's for exclusive distribution. Don't you remember?"

"Oh, of course I remember what you said, sweetheart," David answered, "but I knew you didn't mean it. You were angry that day. I knew once you calmed down you'd—"

"Once I calmed down?" Tilley said in disbelief. "You weren't listening to a word I said."

"Yes, I was," David said impatiently. "I heard every word. I knew you didn't really mean it." He sat down in the chair beside her desk. "Now come here. Let me show you this. You know I'm leaving next week, and I'd like to get at least some of this straightened out before I go. It's going to be hard enough going off without you, though I'm counting on your coming over—"

Tilley put both her hands flat on the desk in front of her and sat down. "David Danforth, you're not listening to me."

"Oh, yes I am," David said absently, looking for something in the stack of papers.

"What you mean is that I was an hysterical, sentimental female who didn't know her own mind. You thought with time I would come around and see the error of my ways. Am I right?" She folded her arms.

David looked up at her, a baffled expression on his face. "Something like that," he said, as if he were just beginning to hear her. "Though I think 'hysterical' is a bit dramatic."

Tilley ignored his attempt at humor. She was angry and getting angrier by the minute. "All this time I thought you understood. I thought you weren't going to insist on something I obviously have bad feelings about."

"Tilley! That's ridiculous," David blurted out, banging

his fist on the desk. "You can't run a business on feelings—good or bad."

"You may not," Tilley retorted promptly, "but I surely can. That's why I'm in business for myself. I'm going to do what I want to do when I want to do it, and right now I don't want to have a contract to be Danforth's exclusive sweetie pie."

"Sweetie pie?" David repeated incredulously. "What do you mean by that?"

"I'm sorry, David," Tilley demurred. "I lost my temper. That was uncalled for."

David softened his stance. "Well, would you just read through the contracts, see if—"

"No, I won't." Tilley was adamant. She had decided to stand firm. "I've made up my mind. I've got my hands full as it is trying to keep up with this business of mine. I like what's happening with it. I like it just the way it is. It's small enough so I can have some control over it."

"You're being a mother hen," David said angrily. He stood up and pushed his hands down in his pockets. "One of these days you're going to realize that you've got an overgrown adolescent on your hands that you don't know what to do with. You can't stifle it, Tilley."

"That may very well be true, David," Tilley said coldly, reaching across the desk for the papers. "I hope not. But then that's for me to decide, isn't it? It's my business, after all." She took the purchase orders out of the stack and handed the contracts back to David.

David took them from her, folded them in half, and stuck them in the pocket of his suit. "I thought we had a

commitment to each other, Tilley. I didn't expect this."
There was a wistful quality to his voice.

Tilley sighed and closed her eyes. Inwardly, she was
seething. "And that's the biggest problem of all, David. If
we have any commitment, it's a personal one, not a
professional one. But you don't seem to make any
distinction."

"That's not fair," David demanded, "and you know it.
What's between us has nothing to do with this contract."
There was cold fury in his eyes.

"Maybe not," Tilley admitted, her eyes meeting his
directly. "Maybe it's that you can't stand not having
every single thing you want when you want it. Maybe the
only reason you're so dead set on distributing my candy
is that I won't let you have it."

"Oh, come on, Tilley. You know better than that. You
make the best candy in the country. It's perfectly natural
for me to want it for Danforth's." There was a knock on
the door. "What is it now?" David said, irritably turning
toward the sound.

"I'll take care of it," Tilley said, getting up from her
desk. "It's not your problem." She walked across the
room.

"Yes," she said, opening the door, hoping her voice
didn't betray her agitated state of mind.

"I'm sorry to interrupt you," Amelia said, looking from
Tilley to David. She seemed to sense that something was
wrong. "But the man is here with the catalogs."

"Oh, that's right," Tilley said, rubbing her forehead
with her hand. "I forgot all about that. Tell him to bring

them back here. I've made a place for them in the closet."

"Sure thing," Amelia said, hurrying back to the front to deliver the message.

"Excuse me," Tilley said to David, "but I've got to get this done."

"Oh, don't mind me," David retorted with some irony. "I don't want to get in the way."

"You're not in the way, David," Tilley said, picking up on his sarcasm, "and this will just take a minute." She was silent while the delivery man wheeled the boxes around the corner. "Right here," she said with a cordial smile.

When the boxes of catalogs were in the closet, Tilley thanked the delivery man and signed the receipt. "Thanks a lot," she said graciously. "This is just what we need." She was doing her best to ignore David, who was pacing the floor, obviously irritated at the interruption.

"Look, Tilley," David said as she closed the door, "I don't want to fight with you. You're the best thing that's ever come into my life." He walked over to her and put his hands on her waist. "You know that, don't you?"

Tilley put her arms around his neck, trying valiantly not to be upset. "I think I do," she said softly, searching for something in his eyes, some change, some small bit of understanding. "And I don't want to fight with you, really I don't. It's just that—"

"I keep mixing up oranges and apples, right?" There was a touch of rueful self-awareness in his voice.

Tilley didn't hesitate a moment. "Right." She leaned

her cheek against his. Did she dare hope that he was beginning to understand her side of all this?

"Listen. You think that I don't understand, but I do. More than you know. These are growing pains you're going through." He brushed a stray lock of hair from her face. "It won't always be like this. You started a small simple business and it's gotten out of hand. I can understand your not wanting to let go of it." His voice was gentle.

His voice was gentle, but Tilley felt herself stiffen. She didn't like the sound of this. "No, David, that's not it at all. What I'm saying is that I can sell my candy better than Danforth's can." She pulled herself free and walked across the room to the other side of her desk. "I guess that's hard for you to understand. You think Danforth's can do everything better than anyone else."

"That's true," he said eagerly, hoping to make his point. "We can. We can make you famous—"

"Stop it!" Tilley all but shouted. "Stop it now, right this minute. I said no, and I'm not going to change my mind. I'm beginning to think my candy company is all that matters to you, David Danforth. Maybe that's what all this is about anyway. Maybe all you've ever wanted from me was a business deal."

"You know better than that," David shot back, his eyes flashing angrily. "I can't believe you'd say such a thing."

The telephone rang, interrupting their argument. They both looked at it furiously. "That's my line," Tilley said, her voice tired. "I've got to answer it."

"Don't let me stop you," David flung back at her, positively seething with frustration.

Tilley picked up the phone. "Hello," she said, listening for a moment. "May I ask you to hold, please? I'll be right with you." She pushed the hold button on the phone. "David, I don't have time for this right now. Couldn't we talk later?"

"I don't think there's anything else to be said," David replied coldly. He stuffed the contracts into his briefcase and put on his hat. "I think you've said it all." He walked to the door and opened it, but he paused for a moment and turned before he left. "If you change your mind, you know how to reach me." And with that final word, he left the studio, slamming the door behind him.

Tilley had never seen David so angry. She hadn't known it was possible. She felt tired and drained. Maybe she just didn't know him. Maybe he was always this way when he didn't get what he wanted. Maybe . . . Now stop this, she said angrily to herself. You've got work to do. She held the receiver against her cheek, her heart beating rapidly. She had work to do, a store to run. He didn't mean it. It was a mistake. He would come back and say . . . But deep in her heart she knew he wouldn't. She bit her lip, determined to regain her poise. She had a customer on the phone, a very good customer. It was an important call. There was simply no time for anything else.

"Hello," she said, her voice cracking slightly. "I'm sorry to keep you waiting." And while she jotted down the order, she struggled to hold back the tears.

9

·ᴀᴀᴀᴀᴀᴀᴀᴀᴀᴀᴀ·

A goblin's face appeared briefly at the window, and a short bear ran down the street. "Happy Halloween," Tilley called out the door at what she hoped were the last of the trick-or-treaters. "See you next year." The night air was cold, and she shivered slightly as she shut the door. A blue norther had moved through Houston only the day before, and Texas seemed to be settling into an unusually cold winter at last.

Winter—the word had such a lonely sound. Like winter of discontent, Tilley thought dully. She hated it when it got dark so early, and now that David was out of her life, every night seemed like an even more painful reminder that she was totally alone. The days since their argument had crept by, and she kept hoping things would get better. Oh well, she reminded herself ruefully, she still had the Chocolate Moose. She went back into the store and shut the door behind her, closing out the dark night.

"Well, that does it for another twelve months," Amelia said flatly, falling into the nearest chair. Her hair was tied back under a yellow scarf, and she wore an orange gypsy skirt laden with gold braid, a white peasant blouse with long full sleeves, and strings of brightly colored beads around her neck. "And not a moment too soon," she added, taking off her shoes and wiggling her toes.

"You've got to be kidding," Rachel groaned as she slowly sank down to the floor, her back pressed against the wall. "Just one year? Surely Halloween doesn't come around that often. Once every two years would be too much." She had come as Big Bird—yellow tights and leotard and a vest of bright yellow feathers. She rolled her head from side to side, relaxing her shoulders.

"What's the matter with you two anyway?" Tilley asked, smiling at their fatigue. She was dressed as a black cat, and her lithe body seemed even more shapely than usual in the close-fitting black velvet jumpsuit. An elegant black satin mask bright with sequins and pearls was pushed back on top of her head, and her cheeks were flushed a becoming rosy hue from the excitement of the evening. "Surely you're not ready to call it a day? It's not even eleven yet."

Amelia groaned and looked over at Rachel. "What do you suppose she's dreaming up now?"

Rachel straightened her legs out on the floor in front of her, arching her back at the same time. "I don't know," she said glumly, "and I don't want to find out—not anytime soon. All I want is a quiet corner to finish my yoga exercises. I'm counting on that to give me the strength to get to bed." She leaned forward, touching her forehead to her knees.

"I wish you wouldn't do that!" Jacques said when he walked back in from the kitchen. "It's not natural."

Rachel turned her head slightly so she could look up at him. "Give me a break, Jacques. You probably don't think it's natural to brush your teeth."

Jacques let out his usual hummmph. "I'm not going to dignify that with an answer." He had a black plastic garbage sack in his hands and was starting to gather up the paper plates and cups that were scattered throughout the front room.

"I see it doesn't take you long to get out of a gorilla suit," Tilley commented playfully. She bent down to retrieve some leftover candy wrappers from the last of the firecrackers. She had been glad to see them go.

"That thing is hot," Jacques said defensively. "Next year, I'm going to think of something cooler."

Rachel snorted affectionately. She was sitting up now, one leg twisted around her hip. "That's what you said last year, but would you wear the Tarzan costume I made for you?" She shook her head solemnly, answering her own question. "Nooooo." She stretched the word out to at least four syllables.

"You call two handkerchiefs a costume?" Jacques asked with indignation.

"Well, you said you wanted something cooler." Amelia joined in the good-natured teasing. She got up and started helping restore order to the store.

Tilley was paying little attention to the easy camaraderie among her staff. She was thinking back over the evening, trying to decide how to rate its success. "I think we had even more children this year, don't you?"

"At least three times as many," Rachel confirmed wryly. She stood up and stretched her arms toward the ceiling. "Though it's hard to know for sure. Some of them are noisier than three adults."

"Oh, come on," Tilley said with a laugh. "They weren't that bad, were they?" She looked around the room expectantly.

Jacques and Amelia exchanged long sideways glances. "Well, now . . ." they both began at the same time.

"Okay, okay," Tilley said, throwing up her hands. "So maybe it was that bad." She pouted ever so slightly. The annual Halloween party was one of her favorite ideas. Since the holiday had become so unsafe, she had decided a costume party was one of the best services the store could provide for the neighborhood. This year and last they'd had quite a crowd.

"Oh, don't have such a long face," Rachel chided her playfully. "They're just giving you a hard time. You should have seen Jacques earlier, prancing all over the store, looking at his furry reflection in the window. The whole evening was worth that alone." She was clearing off the counter.

Amelia sat back down and pulled the yellow scarf off her head, shaking her long black hair free. "This sort of thing builds character, you have to admit." She looked around the room, checking to make sure that everything was back in place. "How does Pepper manage to get out of this? Doesn't Halloween ever fall on his night off?"

"Not if he can help it," Jacques chuckled. "That boy's got real sense." He had returned from the kitchen, a big white box under one arm, his jacket over the other. He put the box down on the counter and started putting on his coat.

"I'm off, my fair lady—into the night," he said to Tilley.

"You're not going to leave without us, are you?" Amelia was back on her feet in no time, all kidding aside. "You said you'd give us a ride."

"That's what I said," Jacques answered with a sigh, "but I can't sit around here all night. Sybil won't turn the front porch light off until I get home, which means she'll still be having trick-or-treaters. And if I know Sybil, she'll have already run out of candy."

"Pshaw," Rachel said with mock scorn. "I saw all that candy you took home this afternoon. Sybil's got enough for two Halloweens." She was buttoning her jacket.

Jacques squirmed uncomfortably. "Well, maybe, maybe not. In any case, if you're going with me, you're going now. I'm an old man who needs his sleep." He was no longer joking.

Amelia gave him an affectionate kiss on the cheek. "Not so old," she said, "at least not in my book."

Tilley hated to see them leave. As long as they were around with all their lively chatter and pushing and shoving, she could forget that David Danforth had stormed out of her office and that she hadn't spoken to him since. Already she was fighting the same old blueness she faced every time she was alone. Try as she might to ward off the terrible sense of loss she felt, sooner or later she was bound to come up against it.

"Your costume, Jacques," she reminded him as he was going out the door. She reached for the big white box on the counter. "You're going to need this again. Next year will sneak up on you before you know it." She handed him the box with his costume in it.

"That's what I'm afraid of," Jacques said with a mock frown, taking the box from her. Then he added in a paternal voice, "You make sure you lock up tight tonight. You never can tell what kind of mischief there might be."

"Oh, don't worry about me," Tilley said, flashing him a grateful smile. "It'll take more than a few trick-or-treaters to scare me."

"Don't take any chances," Jacques warned as he continued out.

When she shut the door, Tilley couldn't suppress a slight shudder, thinking of the night's traditional association with ghosts and goblins. Pulling down the shades on the door and locking up, she chided herself. "This is ridiculous," she said out loud. Looking around the room one last time, she turned off the overhead light and headed into the studio and her desk. She hadn't had a chance to go through the mail, the day had been so hectic, and she wanted to sort out the orders before Pepper arrived. She was expecting him about eleven thirty.

Picking up the big stack of mail, she decided to work upstairs. A cup of hot chocolate would be just the thing, she said to herself as she took the stairs two at a time.

Tossing the envelopes on the coffee table, Tilley went to the kitchen to make the cocoa. She was too tired even to think about taking off her costume, and a few minutes later, she was curled up on the big white sofa, sorting through the mail, separating it into two stacks, one for Pepper, the other hers to read. When her hand fell on the large white envelope, she knew what it was even before she opened it. Her name had been written by hand, and the return address was Danforth's.

She hesitated a moment before deciding to open it. There's no point making a mountain out of a molehill, she said to herself resolutely. It's just a piece of paper. But it was more than that and she knew it. She opened the two envelopes and pulled out an engraved invitation to the opening of Danforth's new London store. Her eyes misted over with unexpected tears.

David hadn't sent her this invitation, not personally, she could be sure of that. She was on the store's mailing list. No doubt hundreds of them were sent out. David had nothing to do with it. But she picked up the envelope again, checking the handwriting, just to make sure. Of course not. Don't be silly, she admonished herself.

She got up from the couch, tossing the invitation on the coffee table as she walked across the room to pull the curtains shut, anything to keep from thinking about David, from remembering what she'd lost. It had been months since she'd seen him—three months and twenty-four days, to be precise—certainly long enough to have quit seeing his face in every crowd. Or so she would have thought. Now she understood that it would take a lifetime to forget David Danforth, if she ever did.

A thousand times she had rehashed their last argument, knowing that she had been hasty and unreasonable. There was a lot of sense in his point of view, she knew that now. But when it came down to the bottom line, she was back where she started. She just wasn't willing to relinquish her autonomy. She didn't want to see the Chocolate Moose swallowed up by the bigger store. That's what all this was about. Maybe some day—in her own time, her own way—they'd work something out. But David couldn't understand that, and he wouldn't wait. She didn't think he'd ever be able to see her side of it. As far as he was concerned, Danforth's was the only store that mattered, and everything else lay in its shadow.

Still, she had considered calling him, thought of making amends. But each time she had backed down, the memory of his fury enough to stop her. If he'd wanted to see her, he could have called or come by. His silence was testimony to his real feelings. She had come to accept that.

She read of David now and then in the newspapers and knew that most of the time he was going back and forth between Houston and London. It would have been hard to track him down even if she'd wanted to—which was so much nonsense, she knew. She could call his office or write him at the store or . . . She sighed. She hadn't counted on the grief, the pain of losing him. She had been headstrong and stubborn. No way would work but hers, and hers alone. She hadn't known how important he was to her until he was gone. Then it was too late for anything except getting through the days, one step at a time, pushing aside the pain, ignoring the loneliness she felt.

She stood with her hand on the curtain, looking down at the deserted street. It was late. Pepper would be here any minute. She had to pull herself together. There would always be reminders of David, at every turn. She had to get used to it. She couldn't let herself get bogged down in painful memories. I have to be stronger than that. I just have to, she said to herself as she closed the curtains.

Just at that moment, she saw Pepper drive up in his battered pickup and park across the street in front of Southhampton Hardware. She watched as he turned off the lights and hopped out of the car, his stride jaunty in defiance of the late hour. She didn't know how he did it, working as many jobs as he did, saving his mornings to write poetry. He claimed to need no sleep, and Tilley couldn't argue with the facts. She was glad to see him crossing the street, so glad in fact that she hurried down the stairs to meet him at the door. Company would make her feel better. Talking to someone would ease the pain.

Pepper was coming in the front door when Tilley entered the room. "Hello, hello," he said cheerfully, his face registering some surprise at the sight of his boss. "You still up?"

Tilley shrugged slightly. "It's been a long night—lots of excitement. I was just going through the mail and enjoying a cup of hot chocolate. Why don't you join me for a while? We can sort out the mail orders while we talk."

"That sounds great," Pepper answered, "just don't

offer me any peanuts. Ugggh," he said, his face twisting at the thought. "That's all I've seen all night long— peanuts and Dracula. You'd be surprised at how many Draculas there are on a night like this." His face was red from the cold, and he was rubbing his hands together, trying to warm up.

"Is it that cold outside?" Tilley asked.

Pepper nodded affirmatively. "And getting colder by the minute. It's snowing in the Panhandle already. We may even have a light freeze tonight."

"Well, I've got just the thing to warm you up," Tilley promised, turning to go back upstairs. "Come on up."

Pepper seemed more than willing to join Tilley in a cup of hot chocolate, and the two of them talked about the party as Tilley put some milk on to boil. Later, as they started going through the mail together, Pepper said, "Man, this stuff is great! Better than my mom used to make."

Tilley looked at him wryly. "I think that's a compliment. At least, I'm going to take it that way."

But something had caught Pepper's eye, and he was stooping over to pick up something from the floor. "What's this?" he asked, a quizzical look on his face.

Tilley realized at once that he was holding the Danforth invitation. She tried to make light of it. "Oh, it's nothing important. Here, I'll take it." She held out her hand for the envelope.

"Not so fast," Pepper said, twisting away from her reach. "This looks like a pretty classy invitation. Two envelopes yet." He looked down at her and raised one eyebrow.

Tilley laughed in spite of herself. "Yes, I guess it is at that."

"And here I thought only wedding invitations had two envelopes," Pepper said, as much to himself as to Tilley. He had pulled out the engraved note and was reading the invitation. "Danforth's London store," he said, his interest clearly piqued. He looked up at her. "Well, are you going?" he demanded, sitting down on the sofa beside her.

"Of course, I'm not going," Tilley answered instantly. "I've got my own business to run, thank you. David Danforth can take care of his own." There was sarcasm in that remark, and Tilley regretted giving vent to her anger. Pepper would pick up on it immediately.

Pepper eyed her thoughtfully for a few minutes before saying anything. "You know that this store won't fall down if you're gone for a few days. You've got a very capable staff who would be delighted if the boss were away for a while." He seemed to be thinking of something else entirely even as he spoke.

"Well, that's true," Tilley began, knowing it wasn't a point she could argue.

"Of course it's true. It's as plain as the nose on your face." Pepper reached for the stack of mail and started flipping through the orders. Then he said casually, "I thought there was something special between you and that Danforth fellow."

Tilley was determined to downplay all this. "Not anymore," she said simply, hoping that would be enough.

But Pepper was more persistent than that. He cast her

a sideways glance. "We all sort of thought it was more than good friends. I mean, for a while there I thought I'd have to start working days what with all the traffic around here at night."

"Oh, you did, did you?" Tilley was taken aback. She hadn't expected this.

"Yeah, I did, and then all of a sudden he stopped coming around. His Ferrari practically made grooves in the parking lot." He grinned innocently, but he was watching for her reaction.

Tilley put her hands in her lap and looked him directly in the eye. "It's been that obvious, has it?"

"Yep," Pepper acknowledged. "I'm not the only one who's noticed either. Amelia and Rachel are worried about you. They came over to the bar a couple of nights ago, wondering what we could do to cheer you up."

"Oh, they were just there to flirt with you. Amelia has a real crush on you."

"That's a red herring, and you know it." Pepper's voice was firm, but he had the good grace to blush a little. "We're talking about your love life, not mine."

"Well, it's not a subject I want to pursue any further," Tilley said, rising from the sofa and gathering up the dirty cups.

"I can see that for myself," Pepper persisted, "but there are a couple of things I think you ought to know."

"Something tells me I'm going to have to listen to this whether I want to or not," Tilley returned sardonically. She was standing in the door to the kitchen, a cup and saucer in each hand.

Pepper grinned knowingly and took a deep breath. "That's right," he confirmed. "That's what I'm working up to." He got up and, taking the cups and saucers from her, led the way into the kitchen. "In the first place, that man is as much in love with you as you are with him. And in the second place, you're both so pigheaded I don't see how you're ever going to make this up by yourselves."

Tilley eyed him suspiciously. "What are you getting at, Pepper?" She took the dishes out of his hands.

"Oh, nothing much," Pepper said mysteriously, "just that David was in the bar a couple of weeks ago asking about you. He comes in every so often, wanting to know how you are. This last time, he seemed really down, and after a couple of beers, he said that you were the only woman he'd ever loved, that he'd been wrong to get your personal affairs tangled up with your professional life. If he had it all to do over again, he said he'd do it very differently." He took the cups and saucers back.

Tilley could scarcely believe what she was hearing. "Why didn't you tell me this sooner?"

Pepper shook his head. "He made me promise not to. And anyway, you know I take this kind of confidence very seriously. Besides, I kept thinking you two would make it up somehow. I'm beginning to see that's not going to happen unless I give you a push."

Tilley took the dishes back from him. "Pepper, quit taking the dishes away from me. I'm going to put them in the sink if you'll give me a chance."

Pepper looked a little sheepish, but his mind wasn't on the dishes. "I guess I'm not very good at playing Cupid."

Tilley studied him for a moment. "I'd say you're doing a pretty fair job of it right now." She reached over and kissed him on the cheek.

"Does that mean you'll go to the opening?" Pepper asked eagerly.

"It's not that simple," Tilley answered, putting the cups and saucers in the sink.

"So what's hard about it?" Pepper asked with a shrug. "All you have to do is call the airport and buy a ticket to London. I'll take you to the airport—anytime, day or night." He leaned against the door jamb waiting for her reply.

Tilley turned on the water, and when she spoke, her voice was soft and wistful. "You make it sound as if London were just around the corner. I wish it were that easy."

"Well, in a manner of speaking, it is. This is the twentieth century, you know. Jet lag only lasts a few hours." Pepper picked up a dish towel and dried a cup.

Tilley looked up at him for a moment. Then a slow smile started across her face. "Sometimes to get what you want, you have to do things in a big way."

"Does that mean you'll go?" Pepper wouldn't give up.

"I didn't say that," Tilley warned. "But I think it means I'm going to think about it."

"Now that's what I call progress," Pepper replied happily. "Boy, wait until I tell Amelia about this!"

"Now wait a minute, I'm not going anywhere just yet. I've got to think about this." But the gleam in her eye meant that she was already thinking about the plan as a real possibility. "I don't suppose it could hurt anything, now could it? I mean, if you're wrong and he doesn't want me to come, I don't have anything to lose."

Pepper considered this for a moment. He was being quite honest. "Maybe a little pride, but that's not so much."

"Not when you consider the risk," Tilley said thoughtfully. "I stand to lose a whole lot if I stay here—a lot more than I ever thought possible." She reached behind her and pulled at her costume, twirling the long black cat's tail.

"Now you're talking," Pepper said gleefully. He walked back into the living room and picked up the stack of orders. "Now, if you'll excuse me, I've got some work to do."

Tilley had almost forgotten he was there. She looked up. "Oh, sure Pepper, don't let me keep you." She walked with him to the door. There was a dreamy look in her eyes.

"I like that faraway look in your eyes," Pepper said, as he turned to go out the door. "Remember, I'm at your service. I'll take you to the airport anytime, day or night."

"Thanks, Pepper," Tilley replied, smiling now. "But if I do decide to go to London, I can take myself to the airport." Something about the determined set of her chin was a dead giveaway.

10

·eeeeeeeeeee·

I feel like the little match girl, on the outside looking in, Tilley thought glumly as she walked through the snowy streets of Mayfair. It was a bitterly cold winter afternoon, and in the hustle and bustle of the busy city street, Tilley felt very much alone, a stranger in a strange country. On every side, people were hurrying along the sidewalks wrapped in heavy coats, woolen scarves, tweed caps, and leather boots, the snow crunching solidly beneath rubber soles. They all seemed to know where they were going. There was purpose in their stride, confidence in their cheerful greetings to each other.

For the first time, Tilley wondered if she were doing the right thing. Suddenly, thousands of miles away from home and the chocolate moose, she wondered if she hadn't taken leave of her senses—flying off to meet a man she hadn't seen or talked to in months. Maybe he wouldn't want to see her. Maybe he'd met someone else. Maybe he'd be angry that she'd done such a fool thing, flying from Houston to London on the chance that he'd want to see her as much as she wanted to see him.

Oh, this was too ridiculous. It simply was not the time to lose heart. After all she'd been through to get here, she wasn't about to turn back now. She pulled her coat a little tighter against the bitter cold and the snow that was getting heavier. Who would have thought that just a few short days ago she had been wearing jeans and a cotton sweater?

She glanced at her watch, pushing up her sleeve and pulling down the top of her black suede leather glove. Almost five o'clock. Another thirty minutes and the stores would be closing. She still hadn't found the street she was looking for. She had studied the map so carefully and thought she knew exactly where she was going. Somehow she had gotten turned around.

Everything looked exactly as she'd expected it to, and the rows of posh townhouses and elite shops on either side of the road made her sure that she was in the vicinity of Danforth's. It was an area in perfect good taste, just the sort of place David would choose for a location. She knew she was close. What she was going to do once she got there was still a mystery though. She couldn't exactly rush up and throw herself into David's arms, now, could she?

Oh, why didn't I take a taxi, she thought miserably to

herself. But she knew the answer to that. Something in her wanted to delay the moment as long as possible. Something in her was afraid to rush this, to make it happen any faster than was natural. Besides, she was still making the transition from one world to another. She needed some time on her own to get used to this world with which David was so familiar.

She decided to stall for a moment longer and ducked into a nearby bookshop. The interior was warm and inviting, with deep wood paneled shelves and books of all types displayed elegantly and invitingly. She browsed for a few moments through tour guides of London, wondering how long she'd be staying. When she'd left Houston, she hadn't told them how long she'd be gone. She smiled, remembering their reactions.

Jacques had listened sagely to her plan, then nodded approvingly. "About time you developed some sense about men," he said with a smile. "I've liked Mr. Danforth from the very beginning. I always thought he could make you happy, Tilley. And if it means following him to London, I think you should do it. We can hold down the fort."

Tilley blushed slightly, and tears filled her eyes. Pepper, seeing her emotion, interjected, "That's what I told her, Jacques. Just because she works all the time doesn't mean she's indispensable."

She tried to look indignant as the twins threw in their two cents. "I think it's terribly romantic," Amelia breathed. "It's like something out of the movies, following your man to another continent. I'm all for it, Tilley.

My midterms will be over by then, and it'll be a while before I have to start studying for finals, so we can work overtime, can't we, Rachel?"

Her twin nodded approvingly. "Besides, it's not a vacation, Tilley. If my memory serves me correctly, you can write the whole thing off as a tax deduction. After all, Danforth's is selling Chocolate Moose candy. So even if it doesn't work out the way you hope it does, you won't be out anything," she added practically.

Everyone burst out laughing. "You have the soul of a calculator," Amelia said reprovingly.

Rachel looked slightly offended, then gave her sister a teasing glance. "I guess I just got all the mathematically inclined genes, Sis. I know you can't add two and two."

"Now, now," Tilley said, not wanting them to fight. "It really doesn't matter. The two of you do different things and you do them wonderfully, each of you in your own way. And I appreciate both of you. I'm especially glad that my being gone won't interfere with your studies."

"Not mine," Rachel said proudly, giving Amelia a pointed glance.

"Mine either," Amelia said quickly and defensively.

"Great, then that settles it," Tilley said firmly, not wanting to give herself a chance to back out now. "I'll call the airline and make a reservation."

She'd called David's office first, however, just to make sure he wasn't coming home before the opening. She didn't want to fly all the way over there just to find out he was in Houston. But she was told that Mr. Danforth wouldn't be back until Christmas. At least those were his intentions, his secretary said. Then Tilley called the airport. But that hadn't been quite as easy as she'd thought it would be. In the end, she had to wait a few days even to get on the standby list. It seemed like everyone wanted to go to London for Thanksgiving. And though the opening wasn't for another ten days, Tilley was afraid she might end up missing it, not because she hadn't tried. She thanked heaven for the passport she'd gotten a long time ago, thinking that when she left Wall Street she'd take off on a European vacation.

Pepper had driven her to the airport after all. He insisted, saying that it was the closest he'd ever get to England. He waited in the airport lounge with her while she lingered in suspense, hoping she'd make the flight. He'd spent two hours entertaining her with bartender stories, and when the reservations clerk called her name, he'd walked her to the ticket counter and given her a fierce hug. "Go get 'em, Tilley!" he muttered. "I'm proud of you for going. And remember—we don't expect you to come back empty-handed. You have a good time. And if you get worried about the business, just call. That's what telephones are for."

Tilley had laughed at the prospect. "Hey, Pepper, you guys can handle it. I taught you well, remember? You just make sure that nobody works too hard while I'm off jaunting around on red doubledecker buses, okay?"

He had laughed and let her go, and when Tilley walked through the jetway to board the plane, she had turned to wave goodbye. Pepper, the optimistic romantic, gave her a thumbs-up sign and walked away.

"May I serve you, miss?"

The voice of the bookshop clerk broke sharply into her reverie. With a start, Tilley realized that she was thousands of miles away from Jacques and Pepper, Amelia and Rachel, her whole world, in fact. And she'd come here for only one reason—to see David. So why was she putting it off? She gave the red-cheeked Englishwoman a broad smile. "Yes, I'd like these," she said, handing her the two guidebooks she held in her hand. If David didn't have time to show her London, she'd see it on her own.

She paid for the guidebooks with the unfamiliar bills and coins, grateful that she'd been able to change money at her small Bloomsbury hotel. Her training in economics had made her relatively familiar with the rate of exchange, and she'd even managed the Underground that morning, with a few directions from the hotel desk clerk. Really, it hadn't been at all difficult. So why was she making it so hard now?

As she walked toward the front door of the bookshop, she turned back toward the clerk who'd waited on her and asked for directions to Danforth's.

"Oh, yes, miss," the clerk assured her. "It's up two blocks, then take a left. They have the most marvelous windows. You can't miss it."

Tilley squared her shoulders and marched out into the snow. It was now or never. She walked briskly along the street, and this time her stride was purposeful. She turned the corner where the clerk had told her and stood stock still, heedless of the excited shoppers bustling past her. The clerk had been right. Danforth's did have marvelous windows. She would have known them anywhere.

Directly ahead of her was a brilliantly lit display window with a cheery Santa sitting in a red, white, and blue sleigh, pulled by a team of chocolate moose. It was exactly the way David had described it to her, but she had never dreamed it would be so appealing, would look so clever. The red, white, and blue sleigh clearly announced that the Americans had arrived in London. She smiled, thinking of the pleasure David must be taking in this store, and she had the sudden impulse to rush forward and join him. She'd already wasted enough time.

As she hurried across the street, she realized that the window wasn't empty. Someone was bent over, adjusting the Santa Claus. All she could see behind the red figure was the top of a head. But as she moved closer, she knew immediately who it was in the window. He looked exactly as she remembered, the determined tilt of his chin, the stoop of his shoulders as he lifted the Santa into the sleigh, his movements graceful as he worked. He was wearing dark slacks and a green sweater, the sleeves pushed up to his elbows.

Suddenly Tilley was shy. She was so close to the window that she could reach out and touch it. She stopped short, afraid to move another step, afraid to disturb his concentration. She didn't know what she was going to do next. The sidewalk around her was crowded with late afternoon shoppers brushing past her, jostling her. The snow was falling heavily now, and she could feel it touch her cheeks.

But it wasn't long before David realized someone was watching him. Or maybe he just happened to look up. Tilley was never sure what happened. But he did look up, and his eyes fell on her as if he had known she would be standing there, had known it all along.

For a moment, time stood still. Neither moved or blinked an eyelash, and yet it seemed to Tilley that David had taken her into his arms, held her close, tight, a silent promise never to let her go again. She felt her knees weaken, her cheeks blush, her heart sing out for joy, and when time took over once again, her hands were flat on the window, only glass separating her palms from his.

"Tilley!" he called out through the thick glass. Looking down at her for a long searching moment, his eyes reflected a myriad of emotions—curiosity, excitement, relief, and most of all, love. Love. That's what Tilley saw there, and she berated herself for having been blind to it for so long.

"Wait right there," she could hear him say faintly. And then he was gone. But she couldn't wait, not after all these months. She turned and ran along the sidewalk until she came to a revolving glass door. She half expected it to be locked, but when her hands touched the metal bar, the door moved and she was spinning around, around, straight into the arms of the man she loved.

"Oh, Tilley," he said hoarsely, his lips brushing against

her hair as he held her tight against his chest. "You came. You really did. When I sent you the invitation, I was afraid you'd throw it away. I never thought for a minute—"

Tilley pulled back, looking at him in astonishment. "You mean *you* sent that invitation?" She was incredulous.

David was nonplussed. "Of course, I did. Who else would have sent it to you?"

Tilley shook her head, laughing gently. "I thought it was your handwriting, but then I thought I was seeing things that weren't there, wishing for something I'd lost. I thought . . . oh, never mind what I thought. It doesn't matter now." And as she smiled up at him, she knew that he was going to kiss her. Nothing else seemed to matter. She was home—safe and sound—in the arms of David Danforth, the man she belonged with. And she wasn't ever going to leave him again, not even if it meant chasing him halfway around the world. His lips lingered on hers, claiming her, reminding her of the love that they shared.

When they broke apart, David looked down at her and said softly, "Nothing else matters, nothing except that we never be separated again."

Tilley was about to reply when there was a smattering of applause from around the room. Startled, Tilley looked around. Though the store wasn't officially open, it was full of salespeople and workmen putting on the finishing touches—painting a sign, dressing a mannequin, arranging row after row of glass counters. Tilley felt her cheeks redden as she realized they had an audience. As far as she had been concerned, she and David were the only two people in the world.

But David didn't seem in the least bit embarrassed. Instead, putting his arm around her shoulder and turning toward the small crowd gathered at the foot of the escalator, he introduced her. "This, my friends, is the lady who makes the chocolate moose candy—Tilley Hart, the sweetest temptation in the store. We're going to be married, as soon as possible, maybe sooner." He looked down at Tilley and grinned. "Or do I take too much for granted?"

"No, Mr. Danforth, you don't take too much for granted. That's why I'm here." The applause broke out again, this time with even more enthusiasm. One of the workmen in paint-spattered coveralls was the first to come over and shake her hand.

"I must say," the English voice announced, "I thought that all the best candy in the world was made in England. But that chocolate moose candy is the best I've ever tasted. Mr. Danforth here has to practically keep it under lock and key."

"Now Charlie, you know that's not true," David began, but Tilley didn't give him a chance to finish his sentence.

"Why, thank you," Tilley said with genuine gratitude. "And what is your name?"

"Charlie. Charlie Poole. I'm the one that's doing all the windows, at least those that I can get Mr. Danforth out of."

"Good show, that," another voice interrupted. "So

this is the elusive Ms. Hart that David talks so much about." A ruddy-faced man with a tape measure around his neck gave her a warm handshake.

David spoke up. "Tilley, this is the best tailor in all of England, Michael Ainsworth." The two men obviously had a close, affectionate relationship.

"I've worked for Mr. Danforth ever since the idea for Danforth's in London ever came up. Knew him as a lad when he was working his way up over at Harrod's. He's told me a good bit about you, and from the looks of it, it's all true."

"Now, now, Mike," David said, pulling Tilley close to his side. "Don't fill her head full of ideas. And don't get any yourself. This lady definitely belongs with this gentleman," he concluded, tapping himself on the chest.

"Definitely!" Tilley echoed, giving David a smile. "If the lady hadn't thought so, she wouldn't have flown all the way to London just to see him."

David gave his friend a knowing nod, indicating that he wanted some time alone with Tilley. Then he pulled her off under the escalator where they could have some privacy. "When did you get here? Why did you decide to come?" The questions all came tumbling out in a rush, and Tilley didn't know where to begin. It suddenly seemed that she had so very much to tell him.

"I took a lesson from you, my friend," she said, a mysterious grin on her face.

"What's that?" David seemed genuinely puzzled.

"If you want something enough, you have to do things in a big way," Tilley said proudly.

David threw back his head and roared. "Well, I'm glad to see that I was good for something," he said, looking down at her tenderly. He reached out to gather her into his arms once again. "I sure said a bunch of crazy things. I'd hate to think you'd taken all of them to heart."

Tilley put her arms around his neck. "Enough to know how wrong I've been—about lots of things. Oh, David, I was so stubborn and hard-headed. You were right, of course, I've been too much of a mother hen to the Chocolate Moose. It's time I started letting go of some of it. It's just that it's always been all I had and—"

David put his finger over her lips, shushing her. "I've been wrong about so many things that it might take us the rest of the night just to list them. But the main thing, Tilley, I want you to know right up front—I've come to realize that I've got a store and you've got a store and neither one of them has anything to do with you and me. You need to run your business the way you see fit, and I'll do the same. I was wrong to insist that you let Danforth's be your exclusive distributor. That's a decision you have to make—and, I might add, I can see a lot of reasons you might be better off just as you are. I've got to stop judging the rest of the world by what it can do for Danforth's."

"My goodness, that's practically a speech," Tilley teased playfully. "You seem to know what you're talking about."

"I ought to," David replied evenly, "I've been rehearsing it for the past four months and—"

"Three days," Tilley finished for him. "It's been a long

time, David," she whispered, her eyes misting over with tears. She could feel his heart racing as she nestled closer into the soft wool of his sweater.

"Too long," David concurred, brushing a tear from the corner of her eye. He leaned down to kiss her hair and held her tightly, as if he were inhaling her very presence.

"We don't have to decide all this right now, do we?" Tilley asked a little plaintively. "Can't we work all this out later—say, over dessert?" There could be no hiding the mirth in her voice.

"I think that can be arranged," David said, giving her another hug. "Oh, Tilley," he said, his lips warm against her cheek. "This is almost too good to be true."

"Do you want me to pinch you?" Tilley asked innocently. "Maybe you're dreaming."

"Don't you ever take anything seriously?" David returned with a mock pout.

Tilley's eyes widened. "I take everything you say seriously, David Danforth—even some of the things you don't say."

"Now what does that mean?" David asked indignantly, holding her at arm's length and cocking his head to one side.

"Well, for starters, you haven't told me you love me yet," she replied, her lips puckered slightly.

The truth began to dawn on David, and his whole face registered the impact. "I haven't, have I?" he said to her. It wasn't really a question.

"No," Tilley responded, her face straight.

"Is it too late?" he asked, the laugh lines crinkling around the corners of his eyes.

"You know better than that," Tilley said softly.

"I love you, Tilley Hart, with all my heart and soul."

"And I love you, always and forever," Tilley answered, a satisfied smile on her face.

"Surely you already knew it, even without my saying it?" David said earnestly. He seemed to want to make sure.

Tilley nodded affirmatively. "I knew it for sure when I saw you standing in the window, fixing that Santa Claus. Your eyes said that and more." She ruffled his hair affectionately with her hand. She looked more beautiful than ever, her dark brown eyes filled with happiness, her cheeks flushed with the glow of success. She had done the right thing after all in coming to London. Now she could relax.

David pushed a stray tendril from her face and sighed deeply. "I want you all to myself," he said hoarsely. "What do you say we get out of here?"

Tilley tossed her head, realizing again where they were. "But David, I haven't even seen the store yet," she protested.

"Ms. Hart, you've got the rest of your life to see this store. I think the grand tour can wait until tomorrow." David had already taken her by the hand, and they were walking to the door.

"You're sure I'm not taking you away from something you need to do? I know how important this opening is to you and—"

"You're not taking me away from anything," David insisted, pushing through the revolving door. "These folks are about to close up for the night anyway. You and

I are going to Fortnum's in Piccadilly and have a real English tea and a real American heart-to-heart." He put two fingers between his teeth and whistled for a taxi. "Then we're going straight to the American Embassy."

Tilley knew what Fortnum & Mason's was, for she'd read about the elegant food emporium for years, but she couldn't imagine why they'd need to go to the American Embassy. "But what for?" she asked. "Some last-minute detail for the opening?"

"You might say that," David said smugly. He waved the taxi over to the curb. "I've got to find out how two Americans can get married in this country! That's at the top of my list right now."

"Now? Right this minute?" Tilley brushed snow from her face. She stepped closer to David who was standing on the curb, waiting until the taxi stopped. "Are you sure?" There was so much noise on the street that they had to practically shout to be heard.

"Sure as I can be," David said. "Once I make up my mind that I want something, I go after it." He looked down at Tilley with a grin. "And all I have in mind right now is a whirlwind London wedding. And I think you know that what I want, I usually get." He held open the door for her.

"I'm glad you do," Tilley said, her eyes filled with wonder, "and as long as what you want is me, I guess that's all right." She shivered as she climbed into the waiting taxi.

David climbed in beside her and took her in his arms. "Tilley," he said, his voice very serious, "I'll always want you. You know that. We'll make it work—even if I have to help Jacques make chocolate moose, we'll make it work. All the time. Our lives will be a real adventure, I promise you that."

Tilley's blood raced with excitement. Their time together had already been an adventure. It could only get better. She chuckled a bit at the prospect of David making candy in the kitchen with Jacques. Who knew? Anything was possible. "So what are you waiting for?" she demanded saucily. "Let's get started on this adventure."

"I'd be glad to, lady, if you'd just tell me where to go," a surly voice growled from the front seat. The driver didn't even look around.

Tilley giggled, covering her mouth with her hand.

"We want to go to Fortnum's in Piccadilly," David told the driver as he put his arm around Tilley and settled back against the seat.

The taxi shot into the traffic with a lurch.

Tilley broke away from David long enough to reach forward and tap the driver on the shoulder. "No, we don't!" she said firmly. David looked at her in surprise.

"We want to go to the American Embassy—as quickly as possible."

The driver shook his head, as if to say, "Americans," and began driving again.

"No tea?" David asked mischievously.

"No tea," Tilley said. "That can wait. Other things are more important. And we don't need to make any plans. We know what we're doing. Besides, it's what I want. And like you, David Danforth, once I make up my mind that I want something, I usually get it."

"I'll make sure you do in the future," David promised, and Tilley knew that he was promising much more than that. They both looked out at the snowy London day and exchanged a glance filled with love and hope. The adventure had already begun.

If you've enjoyed this book, mail this coupon and get 4 thrilling

Silhouette Desire®

novels FREE (a $7.80 value)

If you've enjoyed this Silhouette Desire novel, you'll love the 4 <u>FREE</u> books waiting for you! They're yours as our gift to introduce you to our home subscription service.

Get Silhouette Desire novels before they're available anywhere else.

Through our home subscription service, you can get Silhouette Desire romance novels regularly—delivered right to your door! Your books will be *shipped to you two months before they're available anywhere else*—so you'll never miss a new title. Each month we'll send you 6 new books to look over for 15 days, without obligation. If not delighted, simply return them and owe nothing. Or keep them and pay only $1.95 each. There's no charge for postage or handling. And there's no obligation to buy anything at any time. You'll also receive a subscription to the Silhouette Books Newsletter *absolutely free!*

So don't wait. To receive your four FREE books, fill out and mail the coupon below *today!*

SILHOUETTE DESIRE and colophon are registered trademarks and a service mark of Simon & Schuster, Inc.

YOU'LL BE SWEPT AWAY WITH SILHOUETTE DESIRE

$1.75 each

1 ☐ James
2 ☐ Monet
3 ☐ Clay
4 ☐ Carey

5 ☐ Baker
6 ☐ Mallory
7 ☐ St. Claire

8 ☐ Dee
9 ☐ Simms
10 ☐ Smith

$1.95 each

11 ☐ James
12 ☐ Palmer
13 ☐ Wallace
14 ☐ Valley
15 ☐ Vernon
16 ☐ Major
17 ☐ Simms
18 ☐ Ross
19 ☐ James
20 ☐ Allison
21 ☐ Baker
22 ☐ Durant
23 ☐ Sunshine
24 ☐ Baxter
25 ☐ James
26 ☐ Palmer
27 ☐ Conrad
28 ☐ Lovan
29 ☐ Michelle

30 ☐ Lind
31 ☐ James
32 ☐ Clay
33 ☐ Powers
34 ☐ Milan
35 ☐ Major
36 ☐ Summers
37 ☐ James
38 ☐ Douglass
39 ☐ Monet
40 ☐ Mallory
41 ☐ St. Claire
42 ☐ Stewart
43 ☐ Simms
44 ☐ West
45 ☐ Clay
46 ☐ Chance
47 ☐ Michelle
48 ☐ Powers

49 ☐ James
50 ☐ Palmer
51 ☐ Lind
52 ☐ Morgan
53 ☐ Joyce
54 ☐ Fulford
55 ☐ James
56 ☐ Douglass
57 ☐ Michelle
58 ☐ Mallory
59 ☐ Powers
60 ☐ Dennis
61 ☐ Simms
62 ☐ Monet
63 ☐ Dee
64 ☐ Milan
65 ☐ Allison
66 ☐ Langtry
67 ☐ James

68 ☐ Browning
69 ☐ Carey
70 ☐ Victor
71 ☐ Joyce
72 ☐ Hart
73 ☐ St. Clair
74 ☐ Douglass
75 ☐ McKenna
76 ☐ Michelle
77 ☐ Lowell
78 ☐ Barber
79 ☐ Simms
80 ☐ Palmer
81 ☐ Kennedy
82 ☐ Clay
83 ☐ Chance
84 ☐ Powers
85 ☐ James
86 ☐ Malek

YOU'LL BE SWEPT AWAY WITH SILHOUETTE DESIRE

$1.95 each

87 ☐ Michelle	105 ☐ Blair	123 ☐ Paige	141 ☐ Morgan
88 ☐ Trevor	106 ☐ Michelle	124 ☐ St. George	142 ☐ Nicole
89 ☐ Ross	107 ☐ Chance	125 ☐ Caimi	143 ☐ Allison
90 ☐ Roszel	108 ☐ Gladstone	126 ☐ Carey	144 ☐ Evans
91 ☐ Browning	109 ☐ Simms	127 ☐ James	145 ☐ James
92 ☐ Carey	110 ☐ Palmer	128 ☐ Michelle	146 ☐ Knight
93 ☐ Berk	111 ☐ Browning	129 ☐ Bishop	147 ☐ Scott
94 ☐ Robbins	112 ☐ Nicole	130 ☐ Blair	148 ☐ Powers
95 ☐ Summers	113 ☐ Cresswell	131 ☐ Larson	149 ☐ Galt
96 ☐ Milan	114 ☐ Ross	132 ☐ McCoy	150 ☐ Simms
97 ☐ James	115 ☐ James	133 ☐ Monet	151 ☐ Major
98 ☐ Joyce	116 ☐ Joyce	134 ☐ McKenna	152 ☐ Michelle
99 ☐ Major	117 ☐ Powers	135 ☐ Charlton	153 ☐ Milan
100 ☐ Howard	118 ☐ Milan	136 ☐ Martel	154 ☐ Berk
101 ☐ Morgan	119 ☐ John	137 ☐ Ross	155 ☐ Ross
102 ☐ Palmer	120 ☐ Clay	138 ☐ Chase	156 ☐ Corbett
103 ☐ James	121 ☐ Browning	139 ☐ St. Claire	
104 ☐ Chase	122 ☐ Trent	140 ☐ Joyce	

SILHOUETTE DESIRE, Department SD/6
1230 Avenue of the Americas
New York, NY 10020

Please send me the books I have checked above. I am enclosing $_____
(please add 75¢ to cover postage and handling. NYS and NYC residents please
add appropriate sales tax). Send check or money order—no cash or C.O.D.'s
please. Allow six weeks for delivery.

NAME_____

ADDRESS_____

CITY_____STATE/ZIP_____

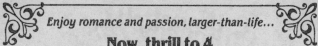

Silhouette Desire

Coming Next Month

The Rawhide Man by Diana Palmer

Bess had always thought of Jude as rough and hard as rawhide—then she discovered another side of him. Their marriage was one of convenience, but then Jude unexpectedly captured her heart.

Rapture Of The Deep by Barbara Cameron

Lori poured all the affection she found hard to express into her work with dolphins—until Jordan pirated her away to the high seas! How had he known she would be able to abandon herself to love there as she never could on shore?

Velvet Is For Lovers by Edith St. George

Alyson was all set to go diving for the sunken galleon—but she didn't know her greatest challenge on the expedition would be its leader, Ivan Kyriokos. Soon she found herself looking for the most important treasure of all—his love!

Moon On East Mountain by Hope McIntyre

City planner Clover McBain clashed by day with Roarke Deveraux over their excavations, but the Korean nights found them unable to resist one another's arms. Could the wisdom of the ages show them the peace that lies in loving compromise?

Through Laughter And Tears by Marie Nicole

Sam had always used humor to mask her feelings of inadequacy—but her armor failed her with talent agent Jake Benedict. He saw right through her, but she *had* to keep him from finding out that, more than his client, she wanted to be his woman.

Dream Builder by Naomi Horton

Lindsay's independence had come at a high price, but she had learned to survive without Ryan—and without love—until he suddenly walked back into her life. Dark and moody Ryan had broken her heart once; did she dare trust him with it again?